A DEADLY CHANGE OF POWER

•

Gina Cresse

AVALON BOOKS
NEW YORK

PRINTED IN THE UNITED STATES OF AMERICA
ON ACID-FREE PAPER
BY HADDON CRAFTSMEN, BLOOMSBURG, PENNSYLVANIA

For Aunt Carol,
who would give anything to have my Dad invent this engine.

Prologue

Heavy brown smog hung thick over Los Angeles as Melvin Oakhurst coasted down the freeway off-ramp and rolled to a stop behind a shiny new 1967 Ford Mustang. A web of electrical power lines littered the skyline. Melvin's sixteen-year-old son, Lance, sat in the passenger seat of the old pick up with his arm hanging out the window, holding on to the side mirror in case it decided to fall off, as it had a habit of doing whenever Melvin didn't shift just right. Lance gazed at the polished car and watched as the blond in the driver's seat used the rear-view mirror to apply her lipstick, probably the same candy-apple red as her new car. Lance almost drooled.

"That's the car I want, right there," Lance said. "John's brother says they're faster than anything on the road."

Six-year-old Veronica sat in between her brother and father. She stretched as tall as she could to see the car through the crack in the windshield of the old pickup. The crack

1

had been there for as long as she could remember, and as far as she knew, Ol' Blue came from the factory that way.

The light turned green and Melvin shoved the gearshift into low. All three Oakhursts winced at the grinding sound. The pickup bucked a half-dozen times before the big rectangular mirror dropped into Lance's waiting hand. He pulled it into the cab and dropped it on the floor at his feet.

Melvin shifted into second and squinted at the mirror. "I'll fix that tomorrow," he said.

Lance rolled his eyes. "Why don't we just sell this old dog and buy a new one?"

Veronica shook her finger at Lance. "Ol' Blue isn't a dog! Besides, new trucks cost too much money. It doesn't grow on trees, you know," she scolded.

Melvin and Lance exchanged glances. Melvin shrugged his shoulders. "Ronnie's right, you know," he said. "I've looked through every gardening book I can find, and not one money tree in any of 'em."

Lance chuckled and tousled Ronnie's hair. "Kid's always right. She sounds more like a forty-six-year-old than a six-year-old."

Ronnie knitted her eyebrows together, pushed Lance's hand away, and tried to smooth her curly hair.

Melvin coaxed the old truck into the gravel driveway of Harold's Machine Shop. The brakes screeched and small pebbles rolled and bounced as he brought Ol' Blue to a halt in front of the roll-up door.

Lance's eyes caught sight of a motorcycle parked across the yard. He piled out of the truck and was halfway to it before Melvin even opened his door.

"Man! Look at that bike! It's a Triumph! I bet it's fast," Lance said, ignoring all but the sparkling red and white racing machine at the end of his tunnel vision. He ran his hand along the polished gasoline tank and sized up the black leather seat. It would take every bit of self-control he had to keep from swinging his leg over and gripping the handlebars, just to see what if felt like.

Melvin lifted Ronnie out of the truck and set her down. She adjusted the vinyl *Flying Nun* lunchpail over her shoulder and pulled up her knee socks. She tagged along behind her father like a puppy into the machine shop.

Harold, the owner of the shop, paused briefly from barking into the telephone to acknowledge Melvin and Ronnie with a nod and a smile. "This ain't the doggone Bank of America, Orville! I won't turn one more piston till you bring me cash. Got it?"

Harold winked at Ronnie, then returned his attention to the man at the other end of the phone line. "Good! See ya later, Orville," he snapped. Ronnie jumped when he slammed the phone down on its cradle.

"Sorry 'bout that, kid. That Orville, he's a squirrelly one. Don't ever trust nobody who won't look you square in the eye," Harold said, as he pushed the big black safety glasses up on his nose. Wispy strands of gray hair shot out of his head in all directions. A metal shaving clung to a strand of hair over his left ear.

Ronnie looked up at Harold with large green eyes. Her red curls were still a little ruffled from Lance's tousling. "Okay, Harold. I won't. You got a piece of metal in your hair," she said, pointing to the curly object on his head.

Harold scratched his rough fingers through his hair until the object fell to the floor. "What've you got today, Mel?"

Melvin shoved his hands in his pockets. "I sprung a leak in my storage tank. I gotta use your welder, if you can spare it for a quick patch job."

Harold gave Ronnie another wink. "Sure thing, Mel. You

know where it is. Just back 'er up over there and help yourself."

"Thanks, Harold. I sure appreciate this. I gotta demo the engine for some big-wigs tomorrow. This could be the one."

Ronnie gazed around the crowded building and studied the complicated machines. Some had wheels with handles and big screws and blades. Some looked like they could bend a car in half, and one looked like it could squash a bowling ball.

Her eyes stopped on Larry, one of the machinists, as he worked at a huge vertical turntable that spun so fast it made her dizzy to watch. There was a large piece of Styrofoam mounted to the spinning plate, and he used a sharp blade to cut away pieces until it looked like half of a flat basketball, only a lot bigger. Larry noticed her watching and cut the power to the machine.

"Hey there, Ronnie. What are you up to?" Larry asked.

"Hi Larry. Dad had to weld something for the magic car. What's that?" she asked, pointing toward the big Styrofoam blob.

"That's Mayor McCheese," he answered. "And over there's Big Mac," he continued, pointing toward a large Styrofoam replica of a hamburger. "A little man is going to wear it in a TV commercial."

Ronnie studied the unpainted work-in-progress. "Where's the sesame seeds?" she asked.

Harold strolled over to check on the progress of the hamburger.

"Sesame seeds?" Larry asked.

"Yeah. You know. Two all-beef patties, special sauce, lettuce, cheese, pickles, onions, on a sesame seed bun. You gotta have sesame seeds on Big Mac," Ronnie explained.

Larry's eyes met Harold's. They both frowned. Harold checked his watch. "What time are we supposed to have it over to the paint shop?" Harold asked.

"Three."

Ronnie slipped the blue lunchpail off her shoulder. She unzipped the top and reached inside. "Will these work?" she asked, holding two acorns out to Larry.

Larry took the acorns from her and studied them closely. "Where'd you get these?" he asked, pulling the little cap off the end of one.

"We had a field trip to the park today. I got a bunch of them," she replied, holding out her lunch-pail to show it was half-full of the nuts.

Larry hurried over to a band saw and cut the acorns in half. He grabbed a bottle of glue from a shelf and stuck the newly acquired "sesame seeds" to the huge burger. "Kid, you're a genius."

Ronnie beamed as Harold patted her on the back. "You just saved the day, kid. I got a Popsicle in the office with your name on it."

Ronnie found a roll-around seat and positioned it so she could watch her father work on the big metal tank he'd hauled from home in the back of Ol' Blue. Harold returned from his office with a grape Popsicle. "Here you go, kid." He pulled a welding mask from a hook on the wall. "If you're gonna watch your old pop weld that thing, you gotta wear this," he said, slipping the big mask over her little head. "Don't want to hurt your eyes."

Ronnie used one hand to push the mask out just far enough to allow the grape Popsicle inside so she could suck on it. A trickle of sticky purple juice made its way down the stick and over her pudgy little fingers.

Larry walked over to get another handful of acorns from

Ronnie's lunchpail. "What's that you're welding?" he asked Melvin.

"It's the storage tank for the hydrogen fuel cell I'm working on. Sprung a leak. I gotta patch it so I don't lose any more," Melvin answered as he pulled a mask down over his face and fired up the welding torch.

Larry gaped at him. "Hydrogen? Jeez Louise!" he yelled as he scooped Ronnie up from her seat and ran for the door. The Popsicle flew out of her hand and splattered on the concrete floor. "Come on, kid, before he blows us all to smithereens!"

Melvin, oblivious to Larry's panic, put the torch to the tank and began the task of patching the hole. Harold followed Larry out the door.

"Relax, Lar. It's metal hydride. He does it all the time," Harold assured him.

"Metal hydride?"

"Yeah. Non-explosive."

Larry set Ronnie down. The too-big welding mask slipped down over her eyes so she couldn't see a thing. She reached her arms out and felt for Larry's legs. "I lost my Popsicle," she said.

Larry raised the mask so she could see. "You know where Harold keeps them?"

Ronnie nodded her head.

"Go get yourself another one."

Ronnie scurried back into the shop and disappeared into Harold's office. Larry followed Harold back inside to get a closer look at Melvin's project.

"What's this hydrogen fuel cell?" Larry asked.

Melvin cut the torch and lifted the welding helmet off. "I built a car that's powered by a hydrogen fuel cell. With this tank, it can run for a month before it needs to be re-charged," Melvin explained.

Larry gawked at him. "Why?"

Melvin pointed out the door at the layer of brown smog that hung in the air like a cloud of smoke, choking the city and everyone who lived there. "See that air?" Melvin asked.

Larry nodded. "Yeah?"

"You're not supposed to. Clean air is invisible. You and I are breathing that brown crud into our lungs twenty-four hours a day."

Larry frowned. "So, this car—it's electric?"

Melvin nodded. "No pollution."

"How many tons of batteries does it need?"

"No batteries. Uses this metal hydride tank instead," Melvin explained.

Larry eyed the tank suspiciously. "What kind of horsepower?"

"Well, nothing to write home about, but good enough to get from point A to point B in a reasonable amount of time," Melvin admitted.

Larry shook his head. "You're dreamin', Mel. Nothing's ever gonna take the place of the internal combustion engine."

"You don't think people will get fed up with brown air?"

"Sure. They're already screamin' about pollution," Larry admitted.

"And what about oil supplies? It can't last forever," Melvin added.

Larry chuckled. "There's enough oil on this planet to keep us going for a heck of a long time. People aren't gonna putt around in little wind-up cars they have to get out and push whenever they come to a hill."

"That's not the case with my car," Melvin said, defending his project.

"Besides, gas is cheap and there's plenty of it. Even if the air turns black as ink, people aren't gonna give up their big-blocks and their V-eights," Larry insisted.

"And why is that?" Melvin asked.

Larry raised the thick safety glasses from his face and squinted at Melvin. "Because, Melvin, everybody wants to go to heaven, but nobody wants to die."

Melvin backed the old blue pickup through the back yard to the workshop he kept behind the house. He'd unload the storage tank later, after dinner.

Jane Oakhurst stood at the kitchen sink, her hands feeling around the soapy water for another spoon to wash. Her apron hung loosely from her shoulders, and hadn't been tied in the perfect little bow behind her back as usual. Melvin eased up behind her and slipped his arms around her waist. He gave her a kiss on the side of her neck and pushed her thick red hair away from her ear so he could whisper some sweet nonsense into it. She didn't respond except to drop her chin lower to her chest, allowing the red hair to fall back in her face. Melvin pulled her hands out of the soapy water and turned her around to face him. Her eyes were swollen and red with tears.

"What's the matter?" he asked.

Lance and Ronnie came racing into the kitchen from outside. They stopped in their tracks at the sight of their mother's face. Both stood, gaping at their parents. They'd never seen her cry before. She couldn't cry. It wasn't something she was capable of, they thought. Even when her favorite cat got so sick and died last Christmas, she didn't cry. They could tell she was sad, but never a tear. Never. This must be really bad.

Melvin let go of her hands and allowed her to turn away. "You kids go play outside."

"But—" Lance started.

"Go outside," Melvin insisted.

"Yes sir," the pair replied in unison. They exchanged concerned glances and trudged out of the kitchen.

Melvin wrapped his arms around her and asked, again, "What's wrong?"

Jane searched her apron for a dry patch and wiped her tears. "I went back to see Doctor Hess this morning. All the test results came back." She broke into uncontrollable sobs.

Melvin turned her around to face him. "What is it? Please tell me," he begged.

She raised her chin to look up into his eyes. "Oh Mel, it's cancer."

He squeezed his eyes shut and she buried her face in his chest. He held her tighter. "Are they sure? It could be a mistake. We should get another—"

"It's no mistake."

Melvin rocked her slowly back and forth and stared at the ceiling. "It's nineteen sixty-seven for God's sake. We've poured so much money into research. We should be able to cure cancer by now. What's wrong with this world?"

Jane sniffed. "Money is hardly ever the answer. Aren't you the one who keeps telling me that?"

He kissed the top of her head. "Yeah, but it can buy a lot of distraction. You know what I'm gonna do? That fella from Standard Oil's been hounding me to sell my patent. I'm gonna call him tomorrow and see just how rich he can make us. Then you and me and Lance and Ronnie are gonna take off. You always wanted to go to Europe. Well, honey, pack your bags. Anything you want, anywhere you want to go, we're there."

Jane backed away so she could see his face. "But you know what they'll do. They'll bury it. They don't want your idea to go anywhere."

"I don't care. All that matters is you. Someday, someone will have the courage to change things, but it won't be me."

It was nearly ten, and Melvin was still putting tools away in the shop. He'd replaced the hydride storage tank and bolted it down in the back of the small car he used to demonstrate his fuel cell technology. The little car was barely big enough to comfortably sit two people. Most of the area behind the seats was reserved for the large storage tank. The car had to be very lightweight to make up for the minimum horsepower generated from the fuel cell engine.

The shop door squeaked, and he looked up to see Ronnie standing in the doorway. Her flannel nightgown hung down to her ankles with ruffles at the collar, sleeves, and all around the hem. She wore the pink slippers Jane had knitted for her last Christmas, the ones with the big fluffy pompoms on the top. Jane made slippers for nearly the whole neighborhood that year. She said it took her mind off losing Snowball, the cat she'd had for nearly twenty years.

"Hey, Ronnie. What are you still doing up? You should be in bed," Melvin said.

"I couldn't sleep." She padded into the shop and let the door swing closed behind her. "What's wrong with Mommy?"

Melvin didn't know what to say. He continued rearranging tools in the big red toolbox.

"Daddy?"

He pushed the drawer closed, turned and picked up the tiny six-year-old. He sat her on the edge of a workbench and pushed a strand of curly red hair from her face. "Mommy's sick, Ronnie."

Ronnie studied his face. It took every ounce of strength he could muster to keep the tears away. He had to stay strong for her. She depended on him. He couldn't fall apart. He'd have to hold the family together.

"But she's going to get better. Right?"

Melvin found a stray wrench that hadn't been properly stored. He busied himself with the task.

"Right, Daddy?" Ronnie repeated.

Melvin clenched his fist around the wrench. He had to keep it together. He couldn't let her down. He would do whatever it took. He'd lie if he had to. "Yes, honey. Mommy's going to get better."

Ronnie let out a sigh of relief. "Good. I was a little scared."

"Don't be scared. Everything's going to be okay. I'll make sure of it. I promise," Melvin assured her. "Now you better go to bed. It's way past your bedtime."

"Can I have ice cream?"

Melvin smiled. "Tell you what. You go in and get a couple bowls and spoons. I'll be right in and we can both have a scoop."

Ronnie beamed. "Okay!"

Ronnie scurried out the door and ran for the back porch. Melvin smiled at the sight of her long curls bouncing as she happily skipped across the concrete driveway.

A hundred moths flitted around the back porch light.

Ronnie swatted at them as she pulled the screen door open to let herself into the house. She turned to see if Melvin was on his way yet. She caught his image through the big window. He smiled and waved to her. She raised her hand to wave back, then jumped at the flash of light. A thunderous boom immediately followed. Shattered glass flew in all directions. Splintered wood and bits and pieces of metal shot through the air. The shop was engulfed in a ball of flames. Ronnie felt the heat on her face. Staring at the fire, she stepped away from the screen door and let it swing closed.

"Daddy!" she screamed. "Daddy!"

Chapter One

Our plane touched down in San Diego at 10:30 on New Year's Eve, 2001. Craig and I wandered down the half-lit corridors of the airport, barely noticing the fact that only one out of every four lights was on. Threats of rolling blackouts prompted officials for the airport to conserve energy wherever they could. We'd read about the California power crisis in the Auckland newspaper, but it didn't become a reality for us until we stepped off the plane.

After three fun-filled weeks of exploring nearly every square inch of New Zealand, followed by twelve hours in the air, neither Craig nor I felt compelled to attend any of the New Year's Eve parties we'd been invited to. We were both too exhausted. We stood at the baggage carousel holding hands and gazing at the passing bags. My own suitcase went around twice before my brain kicked into gear and recognized it.

"Isn't that yours, Dev?" Craig asked me.

13

I shook the fog out of my head. "Huh? Oh, yeah."

Craig dragged the heavy American Tourister off the belt and set it down next to our other bag.

"Thanks, sweetie," I said, leaning in to kiss his stubbled cheek.

New Zealand was our belated honeymoon trip. Now it was time to think about returning to the reality of everyday life in San Diego. Craig would return to his duties as Dr. Matthews and I would pick up where I left off as Devonie Lace, treasure hunter. Oh yeah, Devonie Lace-Matthews. That's going to take some getting used to.

Craig wrapped his arms around me. "I know you're exhausted and you can slug me if you want, but would you mind if we stop by the hospital on the way home? I need to pick something up."

My forehead fell against his chest. "Will you carry me?" I moaned.

"Yes," he replied, and proceeded to heave my 120 pounds over his shoulder.

"No. No. You'll hurt yourself," I insisted, giggling uncontrollably from pure exhaustion.

He set me down and straightened my shirt collar. "I'll only be five minutes. I promise."

I smiled up at him. "Okay," I said, surrendering. I seem incapable of telling him "no" when he looks at me with those beautiful green eyes, and that dimple—Mother Nature's equivalent to a perfectly-cut diamond in a human face.

I tried to convince him before we left for our trip that we should get someone to drop us off at the airport to save the huge parking fee. Uncle Doug had offered, but Craig insisted he wouldn't ask anyone to play taxi driver that late, especially on New Year's Eve. I did the math for him and calculated the parking fee, but he just scoffed. It will take some time to teach him the fine art of conservatism, but I have a lifetime to work on it.

We pulled into the hospital lot and parked in one of the spaces reserved for the doctors. Craig cut the engine but left the radio on. "You want to wait here? I'll be right back."

It was a tempting offer, but I know Craig, and when he says 5 minutes, he really means 25. I'd fall asleep and miss yet another ringing in of a new year. For once, I'd like to at least be conscious for the event. "No. I'll go in. I think Tammy's working tonight. I'll go wish her a happy new year."

Craig led the way into the hospital. A security guard sat on a bench with his back against the wall. At first glance, I thought he was asleep, but when he heard our footsteps, he raised his head to acknowledge our presence.

"How ya doin', Danno?" Craig asked.

The guard gave him a confused look, then cupped his hand around his left ear. "What's that?" he replied.

"I said, how ya doin'?" Craig repeated, only twice as loud.

The guard smiled. This time he heard the question. "Doin' okay, considerin'," he replied.

Craig patted him on the shoulder. "Your hip givin' you trouble?"

Again, the guard cupped his ear.

"I said, your hip givin' you trouble?"

Finally, the guard nodded. "Naw. But my hip is sure actin' up tonight. Must be rain comin'."

Craig and I exchanged grins.

"Danno, this is my wife, Devonie," Craig said, introducing me.

Danno smiled at me. "Debbie?"

"Devonie," I corrected.

"Nice to meet you, Debbie," Danno said.

I smiled and shook his hand. "Nice to meet you too, Danno."

Craig took my hand and led me down the hall. "See ya later, Danno," he said over his shoulder. Danno waved.

"He's got to be three hundred and twelve years old, if he's a day," I whispered in Craig's ear.

Craig laughed. "You might be right. Nice old guy, though."

Craig and I parted ways at the elevator, he toward his office, and I toward the nurse's station.

The place seemed like a ghost town as I strolled down the corridor. I didn't pass a single nurse or orderly as I made my way to the nerve center of this section of the hospital. Televisions lit several of the dim rooms I passed. Most were tuned to the New Year's festivities going on all around the country. I paused briefly to listen.

The nurse's station was deserted—no one in sight. I checked my watch. It was almost midnight. Everyone was probably gathering for an informal celebration in the break room. If I could remember where the break room was, I'd join them. I headed off in the direction I thought it might be, when the silence was broken by a shrill cry.

"Help me! Help me!" a woman's voice cried out from one of the rooms behind me. I turned to see where the sound came from.

"Help me, please! Help me!" she continued yelling.

I scanned the area for anyone who might be able to help her. No one seemed to respond to her pleas. I wasn't sure which room the cries were coming from, but I headed in the general direction, peeking into each room on the way in case I could find a nurse busy with another patient.

As I got closer to the source of the noise, a second voice joined in. "Use your call light, Delores!" another patient yelled out.

"I can't! Help me, Jesus! Help me!"

"Jesus doesn't work here, Delores! Use your call light! We're all trying to get some sleep!"

I pushed open a door, hoping to find a nurse busy taking someone's temperature or blood pressure. I stood in the doorway for a moment to let my eyes adjust to the darkness. The light from the bathroom was on and lit the room enough for me to make out the figure of a tall man standing next to the hospital bed. I blinked a couple times. He wore surgical scrubs, as many of the hospital staff did.

Relieved, I requested his assistance. "Excuse me, but can someone come help this woman? She seems—"

I had obviously startled him. My eyes moved from his head down his arms to his hands. He gripped a pillow tightly against the face of the patient in the bed. "Hey! What are you doing?" I demanded. I felt the adrenaline rush through my system. My hand shook as I groped to find a light switch. He panicked and nearly knocked a tray over as he scrambled to escape. "Stop!" I screamed as he headed my direction. I tried to back out of the room, but he beat me to the door, knocking me down as he bolted past. I hit my head on the floor and was dazed for a few moments.

I looked up to see the silhouette of a man standing in the doorway with his hands firmly planted on his hips. "What's going on in here?" he demanded. He hit a switch that brought light to the entire room. A stethoscope hung around his neck and one end was tucked into the pocked of his scrubs.

"Did you stop him?" I asked, rubbing my head as I struggled to get to my feet.

"Stop who?" he asked.

"That guy who just ran out of here. He was trying to kill that patient," I explained, pointing toward the unconscious woman in the bed. "Oh my God. Is she breathing?" I asked, rushing to her side.

The young man hurried to the other side of the bed and checked her vital signs. "She's fine. She's just asleep. Are you sure you saw someone?" he asked.

I rolled my eyes. "Of course I saw someone. He had this pillow stuffed against her face," I insisted, picking up the pillow from the floor. "If I hadn't stopped him, she'd be dead now." I read the nameplate pinned to his shirt: *Paul Michaels, RN.*

"Well, I didn't see anyone. I think I would have seen him if he was really here."

"Really here? Listen, he was here. I didn't just fall down all by myself. He knocked me down trying to get away."

Nurse Michaels crossed his muscular arms over his chest. "What are you doing here, anyway? Visiting hours were over a long time ago."

"I was looking for someone to help that poor woman in the room down the hall. She'd been calling for help and nobody was answering her," I said.

"Delores?"

"Yes. Delores. She needs help."

"What Delores needs is a good sedative," he said, shaking his head.

I scowled at him. "If that's the case, then why doesn't someone give it to her?"

"Because we have to have a doctor's order, and we can't find her doctor. He's probably off at some New Year's Eve party while we're here listing to a delirious old woman scream all night long."

I turned my attention back to the woman sleeping in the bed. She looked to be in her late 30s, maybe 40. She had a bandage on her head and bruises on her arms and face. I noted the name on the blue wristband: *Jane Doe*.

"What about her? Shouldn't you call the police? Someone tried to kill her," I said.

"Police? No. We have our own security," Michaels replied.

I pictured Danno in hot pursuit of the attacker. "I've seen your security. I really think—"

"She'll be fine. Now, the question is, who are you and what are you doing here?"

His non-concern over this patient irritated me. "I'm Devonie Lace—uh, Matthews—Lace-Matthews, Doctor Matthews' wife. We stopped by on our way home from the airport. I was looking for a friend who works here, but when I heard Delores crying, I started looking for help," I explained. I watched his expression, hoping I'd gained some credibility with my explanation.

His eyes lit up. "Doctor Matthews is here? Maybe he can write an order for Delores."

"What about her?" I pressed, nodding toward Jane Doe.

"She doesn't need a sedative. She's sound asleep," he said with just enough sarcasm to irritate me even more.

"I don't mean a sedative. Someone tried to kill her. She's obviously in danger," I said.

"Obviously?"

"Yes. Obviously. Why is she here? You don't even know her name? How'd she get so banged up?" I pressed.

Nurse Michaels took me by the arm, led me around the bed and out of the room. "I can't give out that information.

You should know that, being married to Doctor Matthews."
He caught the attention of a woman sitting at the nurse's
station and called out to her. "Marge, can you page Doctor
Matthews? He's somewhere in the hospital. Find out if he'll
write an order for Delores so we can have a peaceful night."

I crossed my arms over my chest. "Are you going to call
the police or do I have to do it?"

"I told you—we have security. I'll have someone call
the guard right now," he said, as he turned his back on me
and walked away.

I scowled at the back of his head.

Delores started up again. "I don't want a baby!" she hol-
lered.

"You're not having a baby, Delores," Michaels called
back to her as he headed for her room.

Just as he disappeared around the corner, Tammy came
from the other direction. She'd been working the night shift
for the past month and looked as tired as I felt. "Devonie?
What are you doing here?" she asked.

"Hi. Craig and I just stopped so he could pick something
up from his office." I took her by the arm and led her
toward Jane Doe's room. "What do you know about this
patient?"

Tammy and I had been friends for a long time and I
knew she'd tell me whatever she knew. She peeked in the
room. "Oh, Jane Doe. Yeah, she came in a few days ago.
A couple of sailors fished her out of the water somewhere
between here and Ensenada. She was unconscious for several days, so we couldn't get her real name. No one knows
how she got hurt and ended up in the water."

"Was she in a coma?" I asked.

"Yeah, but she's been in and out of it most of today.
She's okay physically, except for a little bump on her head

and a few bruises. We haven't been able to get her to tell us who she is. She's pretty shaken up about what happened. We can't discharge her until we can find a relative to take her in."

"That'll be pretty hard if she won't tell you who she is," I said.

"Believe me. Two more days of hospital food, she'll be begging to get out of here."

Marge called out from the nurse's station desk. "Tammy, can you check that one? Her call light's on," she said, pointing toward Jane Doe's room.

"Sure," Tammy replied.

I followed Tammy into the room. The mystery woman sat up in her bed, staring at the bruises on her arms.

"What do you need?" Tammy asked.

The woman raised her head and looked at me, then at Tammy. "I'm sorry, but when they brought my dinner, I wasn't hungry. Now I'm starving. Can I get something to eat?"

Tammy checked her watch and frowned. "I'll see if I can scrounge something up for you. How are you feeling?"

Jane Doe gave her a weak smile. "Fine, except for being hungry."

"We'll try to take care of that right now," Tammy said as she turned and headed for the door.

I stayed behind and found a chair in the corner. "Hi," I said. "I'm Devonie."

She gave me a wary look and nodded, but didn't offer her name.

"My husband's a doctor here. The staff is the best. You're in good hands," I assured her.

She gave me a weak smile, then turned her head to stare at the closed curtains.

"Everyone here is pretty concerned about you," I continued, hoping to get her to warm up to me.

"Everyone?" she questioned, still not looking at me.

"Well, I know I am," I said.

She finally looked at me. "Why? You don't even know me."

I hesitated for a moment. "Do you remember how you got hurt? Were you on a boat?"

She remained silent. I decided to be direct. She obviously didn't trust me, so there was no point in dancing around the issue.

"When I came in your room tonight, there was a man trying to suffocate you with a pillow."

"What?" she said with a gasp.

"I walked in just in time to scare him off. Do you recall any of this?" I asked.

"There was a man in here tonight?" she asked, almost dazed.

"Yes, just a few minutes ago. No one saw him but me. He knocked me down trying to get away," I explained, rubbing the bump on my head. It occurred to me that the blow to my head might have knocked me out for a minute or two. That could explain why Michaels didn't see the man when it seemed to me they should have crossed paths.

Nurse Michaels burst into the room with Craig on his heels. "I knew I'd find you in here. What have you done? Did you wake her up?" he demanded, pointing an accusing finger at me.

Craig put an arm on Michaels' shoulder. "Calm down, Paul."

"Did he tell you what happened?" I asked.

"He said you thought you saw someone in here." Craig

scrutinized me closer, noticing the bump on my forehead. "Are you okay? What happened?"

"The guy knocked me down on his way out. Would you tell this person I'm not some lunatic?" I asked, pointing at Michaels.

Craig brushed my bangs back and took a closer look at my injury. "Hmm. Not too bad. I've seen bigger lumps in the oatmeal you fix me for breakfast."

"Very funny. Can you get someone to guard her room? Someone besides Danno? I'm afraid that guy might come back," I said.

Craig checked his watch. It was past midnight by now. Everyone was so concerned with the time. "I'll see what I can do, but it'll be tough tonight. Paul says he'll keep an eye on her. I'm sure she'll be okay," Craig assured me.

"But can you try? I'm worried."

"I know you're worried. I'll call a few people. Wait here and I'll be back in about fifteen minutes so we can go home," he said as he started to leave.

I put a hand on his arm. "That's okay. I'll meet you in the car in fifteen minutes," I said.

He stopped, looked into my eyes and nodded his head. "Okay, fifteen minutes," he repeated, slowly. He flashed me that "I know you're up to something" look, immediately followed by the "but I'm afraid to ask" one.

Jane Doe seemed to retreat to some other world during my conversation with Craig. She knitted her eyebrows together and rubbed her temples as if she had a pounding headache.

Michaels followed Craig out of the room and Tammy made an entrance immediately after they were gone. She placed a banana, a container of blueberry yogurt, and three packs of crackers on the tray next to Jane Doe. "Hope this'll do. It's all I could come up with."

Jane didn't seem to hear her. She continued rubbing her temples and had her eyes squeezed closed.

"Are you feeling okay?" Tammy asked.

"What? Oh, yes. I'm fine. Just a little headache."

"You want me to get you something for it?"

"No. I'll be fine after I eat. Thanks."

Tammy left to attend to other duties. I watched the mystery woman peel the banana. She took a bite, then slid the yogurt toward me. "I don't like yogurt. You want this?"

I shook my head. "Isn't there someone I can call for you?" I asked.

She stared down at her hands and mumbled, "Jake."

"Jake?" I asked.

She seemed to snap out of some kind of trance, peered at the half-opened door, leaned forward and whispered, "Do you think they'll find someone to watch my room?"

I frowned. "I don't know. Craig will try, but—"

She cut me off. "I'd kill for a double cheeseburger. Think you can arrange that?"

I smiled and nodded.

I watched through the windshield as Craig walked across the parking lot toward the car. He had something of significant size stuffed inside his jacked and seemed to be holding it with extra care. He squinted to see me clearer through the glass, then stopped and shook his head. He came around to the driver side and opened the door. He looked at me, then at our new passenger, Jane Doe, in the back seat. "Hi," he said, giving her a warm smile. He looked back at me. "Why am I not surprised?"

I took his hand and tried to pull him into the car. "Come on. Let's go."

That's when I noticed the large black nose poke out of the opened collar of his jacket. Two brown eyes blinked at me. "What's that?" I asked.

"It's a puppy. He hasn't got a name yet. I thought we'd name him after we get to know him a little better. John picked him up for me today. That's why we had to stop here tonight. Happy six-month anniversary, honey."

Craig opened his jacket and pulled the puppy out. It was the biggest puppy I'd ever seen.

"Puppy? He looks full grown," I said.

"He's a Great Dane," Craig explained.

"Great Dane? My God, Craig, he'll be huge."

"I know. Isn't he cute? Tomorrow I'll build a kennel for him in the back yard."

"Kennel? You mean barn. He's going to be as big as a horse."

Craig put the puppy in my lap. He must have weighed twenty pounds. "Don't you like him?" Craig asked.

I immediately received a wet kiss across my face and caught the strong whiff of puppy breath. I stroked his head and held one of his enormous paws in my hand. He was the color of a fawn, and his velvet ears felt like silk in my fingers. "He's adorable. Of course I like him. Thank you, but I didn't know we were exchanging six-month anniversary gifts. I didn't get you anything."

Craig smiled. "That's okay. How about we share him? Sort of like a son?"

I took the puppy's face in my hands and looked him in the eye. The loose skin around his jowls formed a comical sort of doggy-smile. "Hear that? You're our son. We'll have to come up with a name for you."

Jane Doe reached over the seat and patted the soft brown hair on the puppy's back. "He's too cute," she said.

Craig slid into the driver's seat, started the engine, then turned and offered his hand to our passenger. "I'm Craig Matthews. You've already met my wife, Devonie, and our yet-to-be-named son."

She reached out and shook his hand. "Hi. I'm Veronica, but everyone calls me Ronnie. Ronnie Oakhurst."

Chapter Two

The next morning, I called Detective Sam Wright to let him know about the attempted murder I'd witnessed. By the tone of his voice, I imagined him poking pins into a small Devonie doll. He could conveniently pull it out of his desk drawer whenever he felt the urge to punish me for interfering with his well-ordered life. I ignored his sarcastic remarks and insisted he come over to the house as soon as possible. Ronnie Oakhurst's life was in danger, and I'd promised her that Sam would protect her. He ended the phone conversation without a goodbye, and forty minutes later he was banging on our door.

I'd just returned from my fourth trip to the back yard to try to convince the puppy it was much better to "do his duty" outside. He was having a little trouble with this concept, but he seemed to be an intelligent creature, and with time and patience, I was sure he would catch on. In the meantime, I mastered the fine art of keeping one eye on him at all times. I even surprised myself at the speed with which I could cover the distance of fifteen feet—the maximum space I allowed him to get from me when he was in the house. He followed me to the front door to greet our guest.

Sam sat on the edge of the sofa and flipped through pages of scribbles in his small notepad. "Okay. Start at the beginning and tell me everything that happened," he said to Ronnie.

Ronnie sat with her feet tucked under her in the chair on the opposite side of the coffee table. "I don't remember everything."

"That's okay. Just take your time," Sam said.

"Well, one of our sponsors invited us on a yacht cruise down to Cabo."

"Us?"

"Our team. Lance, that's my brother, races on the NASCAR circuit. I was supposed to meet him and the other crew members at the San Pedro harbor to catch the boat," Ronnie explained.

"When was that?" Sam asked.

Ronnie rubbed one of the bruises on her forehead and squeezed her eyes shut. "We were supposed to leave Wednesday morning. What day is it today?"

I sat with the puppy in my lap and squinted to see the calendar tacked to the wall in the kitchen. I'd lost track of the days myself, since returning from New Zealand. I'd lost a day on the flight over, but gained it back coming home. We actually arrived in Los Angeles before we left Auckland.

Sam checked his watch. "It's Monday," he said.

"Monday. Five days lost," Ronnie whispered.

"So what happened at San Pedro?" Sam asked.

"When I arrived, no one from our team was there. I thought I'd just arrived too early, but when I asked around, it turned out I'd missed the boat."

"They left without you?" I asked, surprised that her brother wouldn't insist on knowing where she was before taking off without her.

"Yeah. Well, not exactly. I never really said I'd go for sure. I figured it would turn into a typical party cruise the sponsors are famous for. They bring along more alcohol than fuel. I told Lance that if I decided to go, I'd meet him at the dock. He probably assumed I'd decided to stay home as usual."

Sam scribbled in his notebook.

"Lance knows I'm not a party animal. I'd rather spend my free time working in the shop."

"Shop? Doing what?" Sam asked.

"Oh, I'm sorry. I should fill you in a little more. I'm the lead mechanic for my brother's racing team. I'm the best engine man—or I guess I should say engine person—on the circuit."

Sam stopped writing and raised his eyebrows. "Really?"

Ronnie sat up straight in her chair and raised her chin proudly. "Yes." She noticed the look of doubt on Sam's face. "You don't think a woman can find her way around an engine?"

Sam raised his hands in self-defense. "I never said that. It's just unexpected, that's all."

Ronnie smiled, her hackles no longer raised. "Sorry. Most guys think I look more like a trophy girl than a mechanic. When they find out I have a Ph.D. in physics, they usually turn tail and run."

This time, I raised my eyebrows in surprise. "Physics?

How'd you end up as a mechanic?" I asked. The puppy grew restless in my lap and insisted on getting down. I kept my ears tuned to Ronnie's answer, but my eyes remained fixed on the four-legged toddler trotting around the living room.

Ronnie frowned and twisted a strand of curly red hair around her finger. "I actually consider myself more of an inventor than a mechanic. My father was an inventor. I guess I wanted to be like him, but he died when I was little. He designed steam engines and electric motors and—well, that's beside the point. He was killed before he could teach me everything he knew. My mother died shortly after. Lance pretty much raised me and put me through school. He was racing right out of high school, and he was good. Prize money was okay, but he really lucked out when he picked up a major sponsor. After I graduated, I wanted to pay him back for all he'd done for me. He'd just lost his lead mechanic and I volunteered for the job. He wasn't too keen on the idea at first, but after I made a couple of modifications that cut nearly eight seconds off his best time, he changed his tune."

Sam flipped to a clean page in his notepad. He opened his mouth to ask another question, but I cut in before he could get a word out.

"Who told you what time to meet the boat?" I asked.

Sam scowled at me and cleared his throat. "I'll ask the questions, if you don't mind."

"But it's going to be important to—"

"What happened next?" he asked Ronnie, cutting me off.

I glared at him, and then I noticed the puppy had disappeared into the kitchen. I was on my feet in a matter of seconds to see what he was up to.

"Well, I figured it was just as well. I didn't really want

to go in the first place. Lance has been hounding me to get out more. Anyway, I was on my way back to my car when Charlie offered to take me down to the next port where he knew they'd be stopping for lunch."

"Charlie?" Sam questioned.

"He's the sailor who'd let me know the boat had already left. He had his boat ready and was going that direction anyway. I initially told him no thanks, but I just knew I'd catch nothing but grief from Lance, so I took him up on his offer."

Sam stopped writing and stared at her like she was a two-headed goat. "You got on a boat, by yourself, with a total stranger?"

"I know now that it was stupid, but at the time, it seemed perfectly fine. He was an older man, maybe in his early sixties. He was very polite, and he wasn't pushy at all. I've taken self-defense courses, so I figured if he did get fresh, I could take care of myself."

Sam shook his head and made more notes. "A few judo lessons and these women think they can take on anyone," he grumbled to himself.

I scowled at Sam as I carried the puppy back into the living room and sat down. "You'll have to excuse Detective Wright. He just graduated from the San Diego Academy for Neanderthals, where they apparently don't offer a course in charm."

Ronnie smiled. "That's okay. I'm used to it, working at the track and all. Besides, it wasn't a couple of judo lessons. I hold a black belt in karate."

Sam gaped at her.

She met our curious glances and must have felt the need to explain. "I was mugged once. I wanted to be able to defend myself, and guns scare me, so I took up karate."

I smirked at Sam. "Black belt. I bet she could have your sorry hide on the floor in ten seconds flat."

He ignored my comment. "Did you get this Charlie fellow's last name?" he asked.

"Johnston. Charlie Johnston."

Sam jotted down her answer. "Okay. So you got on Charlie's boat. Just the two of you?"

"Yes."

"Then what?"

"Well, we headed out of the harbor and started down the coast. He said we should catch up with the other boat by about noon, so I found a deck chair and enjoyed the trip. Anyhow, about an hour later, the engine quit. Charlie didn't seem to know what the problem was. I offered to go below and take a look."

"And he didn't question that? If I'm a Neanderthal, then a man born in the forties would have to be far behind me in the course of evolution."

"You know, now that you mention it, he didn't blink an eye. I'm just so used to the guys at the track coming to me for engine advice, it didn't occur to me that he should be any different."

Sam thought about her response for a moment, then made a note in his tablet.

"So the engine quit and you went below to check it out. Did Charlie go with you?" Sam asked.

"Yeah. He showed me where the engine was, then left to find the toolbox. I waited a few minutes, then I heard another boat come alongside. I figured it was a sailor checking to see if we needed help. I waited a couple more minutes, then I heard the boat take off. I thought Charlie must have had a lot of confidence in me to send away a potential rescuer. Anyhow, I kept waiting, but no Charlie."

"You didn't go look for him?" Sam asked.

"I tried to, but the door was locked. I shouted and banged on the door, but he never came back. I hunted around for a key. That's when I found the bomb attached to the fuel line. It looked like a big blob of Silly Putty with wires stuck in it. I took a closer look, then realized I was in big trouble. There was a timer dangling from one of the wires—like the ones we use at the track—counting down from four minutes."

My jaw dropped. "My God. What did you do?" I asked.

Sam set his pencil down and raised his flattened hands in a mock karate stance. "She probably busted the door down with a karate chop," he said, smirking at me.

Ronnie kept a straight face. "Actually, I found a small screwdriver and removed the hinges," she explained.

I leered back at Sam. Here was a woman who could think on her feet in the face of danger, and he was making stupid jokes about karate chops. He seemed a little embarrassed when he lowered his hands and picked up his pencil.

"Then what happened?" he asked.

"I climbed the steps as fast as I could and got to the deck. The bomb must have gone off just as I jumped over-board. The next thing I remember clearly is waking up in the hospital."

I watched Sam write in his notebook. "Now, wouldn't it help to know who told Ronnie the wrong time for the boat's departure? It sounds to me like she was set up," I said.

Sam glared and pointed a finger at me. "Don't even think about getting involved in this investigation. Don't you have some other business to take care of? Oh yeah, a new hus-band. Why don't you go bother him for a while."

Craig's timing couldn't have been better. He pushed through the front door and hurried into the living room.

"Sam, I'm glad you're still here. I just ran down to the hospital this morning to get the scoop on Ronnie's admittance. Bruce was working the ER that night, so he filled me in."

Craig plopped down next to me, patted the puppy on the head, and glanced at each of us. Then his eyes landed on Sam's harsh glare. "What's wrong?" Craig asked, oblivious to Sam's frustration with me and my interference with his questioning.

Sam shook his head. "Now I've got two of you," he complained.

"Two of who?" Craig asked.

Sam dropped his shoulders in defeat. "Never mind. What did you find out?"

"Well, a couple fishermen found Ronnie hanging on to an ice chest floating about ten miles off shore. There was a bunch of debris floating around and it looked to them like some sort of explosion destroyed a boat. They fished her out of the water, but couldn't find any other survivors. They radioed ahead and an ambulance met them at the dock. She was admitted Wednesday night, around nine o'clock."

While Sam was busy writing, I asked my question again. "So who told you when and where to meet the boat?"

"Lance told me. The plan was to spend about a week, heading south to do some fishing and sightseeing. Then we'd fly back home from Cabo."

"No one called to change the plans? No messages?" Sam asked.

Ronnie shook her head. "No."

Sam turned his attention to me. "Can I have a cup of coffee?" he asked.

"In a minute. I have some more questions," I answered.

Sam cradled his forehead in his palms and slowly shook his head back and forth.

Craig took pity on him. "I'll make some coffee. You take it black?" he offered.

"Yeah. Thanks," Sam replied.

"Ronnie?"

"Please. Cream and sugar if you have it."

"Sure. Be right back," Craig said as he disappeared into the kitchen.

"What sort of boat did this Charlie have?" I asked.

"It was big—a cabin cruiser, I think they call it. It was real nice, fancy furniture, lots of shiny chrome."

I looked at Sam. "Sounds like a pretty expensive boat to sacrifice. These guys mean business," I said.

"These guys? You got this one solved already?"

"Would you chill out? I'm just offering my observations," I said.

"Why don't you offer to help your husband in the kitchen? I think I've got this covered."

Craig returned with the coffee. While he occupied Sam with finding a coaster, I continued with my questions.

"Can you think of any reason why someone would want to kill you? Maybe another racer?"

Ronnie shook her head. "There's a lot of competition on the circuit. We're leading in points right now. A bunch of money at stake, but no one is that desperate."

"Don't be too sure," Sam replied.

"So, who's second in points?" I asked.

"Toby O'Brien, but it's not Toby."

"How do you know?" Sam asked.

"Toby's been sweet on me ever since we were fourteen. He'd never hurt me."

Sam scratched his head. "Define 'sweet on you.' Obsessed?"

"No. No. Nothing like that. He's just a really nice guy. He asks me out once in a while, but I'm too busy for anything like romance. Besides, it would probably be a conflict of interest, me working for Lance and all."

"Right," Sam said, not sounding convinced.

Ronnie turned her attention to me. "I have a favor to ask," she said. "I left my car at San Pedro. I really should get it."

Craig cut in. "I don't think you're quite ready to drive yet, but we can pick it up for you and bring it here," he offered.

"That would be great. It's not what you're used to, so I'll have to give you some pointers."

Craig and I exchanged glances. "It's not a dragster, is it?" he asked.

Ronnie laughed. "No. I've developed my own engine. It's very simple. I'll just give you the rundown on how to start it. You won't have any problems. You may want to take along a couple of batteries. It's been sitting for a few days and I meant to replace them before I left for the trip."

"Batteries? Is it electric?" I asked.

"No. You'll just need two double A batteries for the startup fan."

My curiosity was piqued and I could tell Craig's was too. We'd probably have to arm wrestle to decide which one of us got to drive this innovation home.

Sam scowled at me, irritated that his questioning was being interrupted by my conversation. "Great. Now that we have that settled, can we get back to business?"

"Sorry," Ronnie apologized. "Go ahead."

"The first thing we should do is get in touch with your

brother. Any idea where the boat should be now?" Sam asked.

"I'm guessing somewhere around Cabo. The boat was called *The Dream Catcher.*"

Sam jotted it down. "Okay. I'll get on the horn and see if we can find it. We need to know how the rest of the team found out about the time change. In the mean time, I wouldn't suggest you go home. You have any other relatives you can stay with?"

"You mentioned someone named Jake last night. Do you want us to call him?" I asked.

Ronnie shook her head. "He's too far away."

I glanced around our large living room. "She can stay here," I offered. "It's the safest place. No one will look for her here."

Ronnie opened her mouth to protest.

"We insist," Craig said. "Devonie's right. Your face was plastered all over the news when they reported your rescue. Whoever tried to kill you may try again."

Ronnie frowned. "I just can't believe this is happening. I don't have any enemies."

Sam finished up his questioning and left to begin his search for Lance Oakhurst and *The Dream Catcher.*

Craig fashioned a makeshift kennel for the puppy so we could leave him outside while we were away. He stood on the other side of the wire fence and stared up at us with his sad brown eyes. I gave him a little pout. "We'll be right back . . . puppy." I shot a guilty look at Craig. "We have to give him a name. I know. Trigger."

Craig chuckled. "He doesn't look like a Trigger to me."

"No? How about Silver? Bullet? Secretariat?"

Craig put his arm around my shoulder. "What are you implying?"

"That we need to give him a name he's going to grow into."

"I see. And those are the only famous horse names you could come up with?"

"At the moment, yes," I answered.

We turned and headed toward the house. "How about Mr. Ed?" Craig said, winking at me.

I laughed and shook my head. "No, but keep trying."

Craig and I drove to the San Pedro harbor and cruised the parking area. We searched for Ronnie's car, a white Lexus SC400—at least that's what it was on the outside. Craig pulled in next to it and cut the engine. We both gazed at the sleek lines of the sporty coupe. He grinned at me. "I'll flip you for it," he said, pulling a quarter from his pocket.

"Okay. Heads," I called.

Craig flipped the coin and slapped it on his wrist. He slowly raised his hand. I watched his face grimace. "Want to go the best of three?" he begged.

"Sorry, honey. See you at home."

Ronnie warned me the car would be quiet, but I wasn't expecting total silence. Craig and I debated on what kind of technology she'd used. I forgot to ask her if it needed gas or oil or water. She said it wasn't electric, but she never told us what kind of fuel it required. Craig followed me home, just in case I had problems. The car handled perfectly, and it had more power than I expected. In fact, except for the lack of engine noise, I couldn't tell that it wasn't a stock Lexus.

I coasted into the driveway and Craig followed. Ronnie met us at the garage.

I was beaming as I climbed out. "This car is amazing. It's so quiet, and boy does it have some get-up-and-go."

Craig walked all around it, studying every detail. He made two laps before he could no longer contain himself. "Okay. Where's the fuel cap?"

Ronnie laughed. "There isn't one."

Craig scratched his head. "And it's not electric?"

"Nope."

"Well, it must need fuel. What powers it?"

"Heat," she answered.

"Heat? Is it steam?" he asked.

She laughed again. "No. Heat from the atmosphere. It doesn't require any other fuel."

Craig and I gawked at her.

"No fuel?" I said.

"That's right. No fuel. Basically, it's free to run."

Chapter Three

I thought of every imaginable response Sam would throw at me when I told him I was taking Ronnie back to her house so she could pick up a few necessities. That's why, in the end, I decided not to tell him.

Craig stayed home on puppy-watch duty. I told him we were just going to pick up a few things for Ronnie. I didn't tell him *where* we were going to pick them up. That's not really lying. I see it more as saving him from unnecessary worry.

We waited until after dark so we wouldn't be seen carousing around in broad daylight. We took my Explorer in case the would-be murderer was watching the place, waiting for Ronnie's car to show up. She owned a house on a couple of acres in the country just outside of Ramona. I drove and she gave directions. The first thing I noticed was the lack of lights on at any of the homes we passed. It wasn't that late. I would have expected some streetlights or porch lights to be glowing.

"Is it always this dark?" I asked.

Ronnie studied the scene through the windows. "No. I wonder if it's one of those rolling blackouts. They've been threatening us with those for a while."

"Maybe. Or it could be a normal power outage. Isn't that sort of thing common out here in the country?" I asked.

"Power used to go out a lot. I don't know if it's still a problem."

I glanced at her with curiosity. *She lives here. Why wouldn't she know if the power was frequently out?*

Ronnie noticed the look of curiosity on my face. "I didn't like being at the mercy of the electric company. I also didn't like the bills," she explained.

"Tell me about it," I concurred.

"Anyhow, the power went out one night while I was hustling to get some last-minute work done on Lance's engine. We had a big race the next day. I couldn't get the work done, so we didn't even finish in the top three. I was so frustrated, I decided to take care of the problem myself."

"Take care of the problem? How'd you do that?"

"I have my own generator now."

I nodded with understanding. I used to work for a company that had backup generators that would kick in when the power went out. They ran on diesel, as I recalled.

A floodlight, triggered by a motion sensor, turned on as we pulled into Ronnie's driveway and parked in front of her house. She started to open the passenger door, but I stopped her by placing a hand on her arm.

"Wait a minute. Let's just take a look around to make sure no one's watching," I cautioned.

We both scanned the grounds from our positions inside the safety of the Explorer. It seemed deserted, but there were enough shrubs and trees for a potential attacker to hide behind that I felt a little uneasy.

"You're really a black belt?"

Ronnie smiled and nodded. "I am. Stick close. We'll be okay," she assured me.

"Count on it," I said, letting myself out of the driver's side door and quietly closing it behind me.

Another motion-sensor-activated porch light came on as soon as we reached the front door. I listened for the sound of a generator—obnoxiously loud contraptions as I recalled from past experience—but the night was still and quiet. I glanced across the grounds at another house in the distance. It was pitch black. Ronnie crouched down and overturned a dozen rocks in the flowerbed adjacent to the porch. When she found the correct one, she flipped open a small cover and retrieved a key from inside the phony rock. "I knew this would come in handy someday," she said, replacing the rock in its inconspicuous position.

Ronnie unlocked the door and I followed her inside. She turned a small dial on the wall that gradually illuminated the room—a room that spoke volumes about the woman who lived there. The light source came from the ceiling, but it wasn't like any recessed lighting systems I'd ever seen before. Cylindrical tubes protruded vertically from the ceiling about four inches. Each tube was about six inches in diameter and gave off ample light to illuminate its section of the room. The floor was hardwood; neutral tones so any color scheme would work, and easier to clean up grease spots than carpet, I imagined. The leather furniture was a dark neutral color. From what I could tell, Ronnie was not only a problem solver, but also a problem avoider.

A large black-and-white portrait of Albert Einstein hung over the mantle. Posters of brightly colored racecars hung on one wall. I counted a dozen photos of men in racing gear, posing with Ronnie. They all beamed huge smiles, with their arms wrapped around Ronnie's shoulders. Each had a message of sincere well wishes and *Thanks for all the help* scrawled across the bottom.

Ronnie pressed a button on her answering machine. A man's voice casually asked her to pick up the phone, hoping she was just screening her calls. A second message from the same man sounded a little concerned. "I guess you decided to go to Cabo with the team," he speculated. "I'll be out of town when you get home, but I'll call you as soon as I get back," he continued. Ronnie frowned at the machine. I wondered if the message was from Jake, the name she'd mentioned in the hospital.

She walked to the other end of the room and paused in the doorway. "Make yourself comfortable. I'll just throw a few things in a bag and be right back." She disappeared through a door.

I was immediately drawn to a table in the corner with some sort of toy railroad set up on it. It wasn't an ordinary train set. The track had a monorail design. Rather than two narrow rails, it had a single, wide rail down the center. The train didn't sit on the rail at all—it hovered over it. "Floated" may be a more accurate description. I touched the train and it slipped forward, effortlessly. I gave it a little nudge from behind, and it traveled twice around the table before it finally stopped. I was fascinated. I'd never seen anything like it. It must have been built along the design of the bullet trains in Japan. I sent it around the track once more, then backed away to search for other fascinating discoveries. This was like a visit to the Exploratorium.

A shiny, black, dome-shaped contraption moved slowly across the floor at the other end of the room. When it bumped into the wall, it turned and proceeded in another direction, like the toy trucks I've seen racers and their kids play with around the track. It made a quiet humming sound. I watched it with curiosity for a couple of minutes. I had no idea what it was. It looked like an oversized Darth Vader helmet.

I strolled around the room, reading the autographs and studying the faces in the pictures. A familiar name caught my eye—Toby O'Brien, the racer who had a crush on Ronnie. His big-toothed grin spread across a boyishly good-looking face would be irresistible to most young women—women who'd be willing to take second place in the heart of a man whose number one passion would always be the thrill of racing. Ronnie didn't strike me as that type.

Several photos were segregated away from the racing ones. They appeared to be more family-type pictures. Ronnie, together with Lance, whom I'd recognized from some of the racing pictures, sitting around picnic tables, laughing and enjoying who-knows-what. A toddler, identified as Lance by the embroidered name on his jacket, popping a wheelie on his tricycle. A slightly older Lance on a mini-bike, covered with mud from head to toe.

Ronnie came back in the room and caught me staring at a picture of a tall, good-looking man with a curly-haired little girl sitting on his knee. "That's me and my dad," she said. "Just a couple weeks before he died."

I tried to imagine how it would feel to lose someone close at that young age. "It must have been horrible for you, being so little," I said.

She forced a smile and nodded. "It was bad, especially since I saw it happen."

I looked at her closer. "Saw it happen?"

"Yes. He was killed in an explosion in his shop. I saw it from the house," she explained.

"How awful. Were you hurt?"

She looked at me as if I'd asked her if the sky is blue. "I was far enough away," she said, touching the photo with a gentle finger. "But the fear of that pain, that loss, has stayed with me. Then I lost my mother shortly after. I just couldn't take it again. I learned to not let anyone get close to me." She let out a tired breath and glanced around her lonely living room like it was more of a prison than a home. "I'm living proof that time doesn't heal all wounds."

I forced a smile and nodded with understanding. Sometimes the sky isn't blue. Sometimes it's dark and gray and gloomy.

A shiny plaque caught my eye and I quickly tried to change the subject. "What's this?" I asked, pointing toward the brass plate with the words *The United States of America—The Commissioner of Patents and Trademarks,* engraved across the top. Ronnie's mood brightened and she smiled, seeming relieved to move on to another subject.

"That's my dad's patent on the fuel cell engine he developed. My mom had the plaque made for him for his birthday."

I studied the plaque. "Whatever happened with the engine?"

"Nothing. After the explosion, everyone said it was too dangerous to pursue."

"It caused the explosion?" I asked, wary of bringing up the subject again, but wanting to know the answer.

Ronnie frowned. "Depends on who you ask," she said. She turned and walked away. She switched on another light on a desk in the corner.

I peered out a window and still could not see any lights from other houses. "The electricity seems to be on. Your neighbors must be away."

"Not necessarily. I told you, I have a generator," she said.

"All the time?"

"Yes. It's more reliable than the sun and moon."

"But I don't hear it."

Ronnie smiled. "You didn't hear the engine in my car, either. It's the same technology."

"But . . . you can . . . how in the world does it work?" I stammered. This just didn't make sense.

"Have you ever heard of entropy?" she asked.

My blank expression was all the answer she needed.

"Thermodynamics? Heat exchange?"

I shook my head. Computer science majors rarely delved deep enough into physics to understand such abstract terms.

Ronnie pulled a drawer out and extracted an armful of papers. She laid them out across the desk, spreading the bundles until she found what she was looking for. "Here. This is the patent. There's a diagram. I don't know if I can explain it so it makes sense to you, but I'll try." She pointed to a spot on the paper. "Basically, the engine is like a heat sponge. It absorbs heat from the atmosphere and converts it to power."

"How?"

"It uses a piston. Whenever you can create a difference in temperature on either side of the piston, you can cause it to move. The trick is to get heat from the atmosphere into the chamber, then cool it down."

I tried to look like I understood, but I still don't know why airplanes fly, so this wasn't going to be a no-brainer for me. "But what if it's cold outside?" I asked. "Would it still work?"

Ronnie nodded. "It will work as long as the temperature outside is above minus two hundred seventy-three degrees Celsius. That's absolute zero."

What I remember about the metric system is that zero is freezing and one hundred is boiling. I tried to comprehend absolute zero as opposed to regular zero. Ronnie could see me struggling with this.

"Basically, no matter how cold it is outside, it can always get colder. Right?"

I nodded.

"As long as it can get colder, then there can be a heat differential. That's the long and the short of it. I wasn't the first to come up with the idea, but I was able to overcome the friction restrictions, so I could produce more than two or three horsepower. It's as close to perpetual motion as anyone has come up with yet. I was also able to reduce the size so it didn't require an engine as big as a bus to power a small sedan."

"You're a genius," I said.

"Not really. I just like to play. You saw my magnet train?"

I nodded. My eyes widened as I recalled the excitement of my discovery. "I did. It's great. You made it?"

"Yes. It was a project for school. The rail has a positive magnetic charge, and so does the train, so they repel. It's the basis for my answer to the friction problem. You've seen those tacky Eskimo kissing dolls? The ones that will never touch their lips? That's what gave me the idea."

I'd seen those dolls a hundred times, but I never thought to build a railroad on the concept. Ronnie didn't give herself credit. Hers was a truly unique mind—a brilliant mind. "I hope you got an A," I said.

She nodded. "And a few job offers, but I'm happy working for Lance."

The little black machine inched its way toward us. Ronnie walked over and bumped it with her foot, causing it to retreat in another direction. "What is that thing?" I asked.

"It's a bright idea I had that I'm sort of re-thinking. It's a vacuum cleaner. I call it my 'Ugly Little Sucker.' It travels around the house all day, continuously picking up dust and dirt."

I watched it bump into the leg of the coffee table and change direction again. "Cool. Sounds like a great idea. Why do you want to re-think it?"

"There are still some bugs to work out. I've come home a few times and found it had spent the entire day vacuuming the area under the kitchen table because it couldn't find its way out of the maze of chair legs. Then there's the time I got up in the middle of the night to get a glass of water. It had picked up a pair of jeans I'd left on the bathroom floor and strung them across the hallway where I don't have a nightlight. I tripped over them and nearly broke my leg."

We watched the contraption disappear into another room. "I used the same concept on a solar-powered lawn mower. It works a little better. I put a boundary wire around the perimeter of the lawn that keeps it from mowing my flowerbeds or running away from home. It's quiet and it mows continuously," Ronnie explained.

We turned our attention back to the plans in front of us. Bundles of papers scattered on the desk looked like sketches and drawings for other interesting devices. I noticed one titled *Fiber Optic Light*. Ronnie noticed my interest. When I turned my attention back to the unusual lights in the ceiling, she smiled proudly. "Those are fiber optic lights. I came up with the idea one night while I was over at Lance's watching ESPN. He has one of those colored starburst lights sitting on top of his TV."

I nodded. "I've seen them in stores. They're usually next to the lava lamps."

"Exactly. Anyhow, I liked the idea of a single light source being transported to wherever the light was needed. The light at the tips of the fibers wasn't too bright, but I did a little research. I let the idea stew for a while, wondering how I could ever magnify the light enough to make it a feasible means of lighting an entire room. Then I made a trip out to the old Point Loma lighthouse. I read about the special lenses made for lighthouses. They could make it possible for a light as dim as a candle flame to be seen for miles. That was my answer. I had a friend in the glass business make me up a few different shapes for the lenses and came up with those," she said, pointing toward the tubes protruding from the ceiling.

I shook my head in awe. "So you have one light source somewhere in the house and you send light to all the rooms over fiber optic cables?"

"Yes. I have a dimmer switch in all the rooms. Each switch is wired to the main light source, to turn it on when light is needed anywhere in the house. The dimmer switches control lens covers in each of those bulbs to allow the light into the glass chambers, much like a camera shutter."

"Fascinating," I said, turning my attention back to the pile of papers on the desk. I pulled one to the top of the stack. "Is this your design?"

She studied it briefly. "Yes. It's an idea I had for a steam engine when I was in college. It's a closed system. See? The steam is re-condensed and returns to the chamber as water, so you don't have to keep refilling it. It doesn't saturate the atmosphere with water. It only requires enough fuel to burn a small flame to heat this chamber," she said, pointing to a box on the drawing. "This engine could provide hundreds of horsepower and probably travel a hundred miles on a gallon of kerosene or diesel, or whatever fuel you wanted. The best part is that it doesn't require a boiler."

"Why is that good?" I asked.

"Because anyone can operate it. You don't need a special license."

"Do you have a patent on this?" I asked.

Ronnie shook her head. "I had a patent search done. I wasn't the first one to think of it. Some guy came up with the idea years ago."

"Years ago? Who was it? Why don't we have cars using it now?" The questions came faster than she could answer.

Ronnie pulled a folder from the bottom of the stack. "His name's in here, along with a bunch of others. I get lots of ideas, but I've learned to do patent searches first. Most of my ideas have already been registered by someone else."

I took a long look at Ronnie. The ramifications of what I'd seen tonight were just starting to sink in. I needed a little time to process what I'd seen and heard. "Did you get everything you want to take back with you?" I asked.

She nodded.

I looked at the folder she held in her hand. "Why don't you bring that along too?" I suggested.

She gave me a curious look. "Why?"

"I don't know. It's just a hunch, but there may be some answers in there."

Chapter Four

Craig stood at the island in the middle of our kitchen. He was busy filling a cookie jar with puppy treats when I posed my question to him. "What do you think would happen to a person who came up with an idea that could potentially eliminate the need for gasoline?"

He chuckled and continued pouring the dog biscuits into the goose-shaped canister. "You mean after the oil companies got through with him?"

"Her," I corrected.

Craig set the box down on the counter. "You mean Ronnie's engine?"

I nodded.

"Come on, honey. People come up with ideas all the time, but there's always some catch. There's some reason why it won't work. There's got to be. You can't draw more energy out of a process than you put into it. I just know there's something she's not telling us. Her explanation breaks all the rules."

Ronnie walked into the kitchen with the puppy on her heels. "It doesn't break any rules. It just bends a few."

Craig gave her an apologetic look. "I didn't mean to imply—"

"It's okay. I'm used to the skeptics. I don't really care what people think. I don't even know why I let Jake talk me into filing the patent in the first place."

"Jake? You've mentioned him before. Who is he?"

"Jake Monroe. He heads up the research and development department for engine technology at World Motors."

"World Motors? Are they considering putting your engine in their cars?" I asked.

Ronnie let out a half-hearted laugh. "Are you kidding? The day Jake Monroe, or anyone in his position, lets something like that happen, will be the day the temperature in the devil's house falls below thirty-two degrees."

"But why? I thought the whole world was scrambling to come up with more efficient engines," I said.

Craig met Ronnie's glance. "I think I can probably answer that," he said. "*More* efficient isn't as much a problem as *too* efficient. Is it?"

Ronnie shook her head. "No. Since the introduction of the automobile, the number of cars has doubled every twenty-five years. Fuel efficiency hasn't. As long as engines require fossil fuel, oil companies will remain the most powerful entities on the planet."

I was getting the picture. "But since your engine is free to run—"

Ronnie finished my sentence. "Then the oil companies would essentially be on their way out of business. There are a lot of people making sure the Jake Monroes of this world don't let anything like that happen."

"But this Jake, he convinced you to patent your engine? Why would he do that if he knew it would never be allowed to materialize?" Craig asked.

"I don't know. Most of the time, I see him as just another 'company man,' the corporate equivalent of a kept woman. He's wined and dined by all the oil company executives on a regular basis. But once in a while, he does something to make me think he's tired of prostituting himself—like he knows he's in a position to make a real change, if he just had the guts."

I looked at Craig, who was reaching into the bottom of the box to retrieve a stuck doggie treat. "You don't suppose Jake had anything to do with Ronnie's accident?"

Craig looked at Ronnie. "I don't know. What do you think?"

Ronnie shook her head. "Not Jake. He's . . . he wouldn't hurt me."

I thought about her response. "I don't know. Maybe he's taking some heat from all those special interests for encouraging you to file your patent. When you really stop and think about what's at stake, it's mind-boggling."

Ronnie frowned. "It's not Jake."

We were all silent. The puppy sniffed the toe of my shoe, then sat on my foot. I reached into the cookie jar and pulled out one of the puppy treats. "Here you go," I said, putting the biscuit in front of his nose. He sniffed it cautiously, then licked it three times before he finally took it from me and dropped it on the floor so he could inspect it further. "I think he grew since this morning," I said, studying his large frame.

"Sure he did," Craig said. He reached down to pat the

puppy. He playfully tugged on his ears. "This guy's growing all the time. Look at the size of those feet. He has a long way to go to grow into those size twelves."

I chuckled. "Did you get his stable finished today?"

"I did. We just have to come up with a name so I can paint it on the sign over the gate."

"I'm working on it," I said.

My thoughts returned to our original conversation. I felt Craig was still skeptical about the potential for Ronnie's engine. "I want you to take a ride in Ronnie's car," I said.

"Me? Okay. I'd love to take it for a spin. Can I drive?" he asked Ronnie.

"Sure," she replied.

"Good. I'll put the puppy in his new yard," I said.

"You mean now?" Craig asked.

"Unless you have something else you have to do. I want to take you over to see Ronnie's house. There's more potential for her idea than just car engines."

Craig eyed me. "You went to Ronnie's house?"

I nodded guiltily. "Yes."

"After Sam told you not to?"

"Since when did that stop me? She needed to get some of her things. You know how inconvenient it is when you don't have your own stuff."

"Did you see anyone suspicious?" he asked.

"No. Not a soul. Have Ronnie show you her drawings of the engine while I put the puppy out. At least you can get an idea of how it works."

Craig, Ronnie, and I stood in the driveway using the lights from the garage to illuminate the engine compartment of her car. She had raised the hood to show Craig the workings.

"How much of the car is still stock Lexus?" he asked.

"All but the engine and a couple minor changes."

"Really? The transmission? Drive train?"

"All stock."

"Must have been a bear to retrofit your engine to work with the existing mechanisms. Probably not practical to expect the engine to go into cars already on the road," Craig speculated.

"It wasn't hard at all. Just a standard engine replacement. Oh, sure, there are a few little tweaks here and there. I wanted the car to operate like any other car, from the driver's perspective. Mostly it required redesigning the accelerator mechanism."

Craig shoved his hands in his pockets. "But I bet the cost is restrictive. How much to manufacture it?"

"A lot less than a conventional engine, as a matter of fact. It's mostly aluminum and steel. Mass production costs would be a fraction of current costs," she stated.

I watched Ronnie shoot down every one of Craig's arguments. He studied the engine for a few more moments, then put the hood down. "Well, let's see what she'll do," he said, anxious to get behind the wheel.

Craig got in the driver's seat. I slid into the back, and Ronnie sat in the passenger seat. Craig backed out of the driveway and headed for the nearest freeway. "Sure is quiet," he commented.

I leaned forward to get a look over his shoulder. As we started up the on-ramp, I watched the speedometer. "Go ahead. Give it some gas," I said.

"There is no gas," Craig responded.

"Oh, right. Push the pedal. It works just like a regular car," I said.

Craig pushed his foot into the pedal and the car surged

forward effortlessly. Within seconds, we were up to speed with the freeway traffic. "That's impressive," he said.

"Virtually the same horsepower as the stock engine I took out of the car," Ronnie explained.

I could see the surprise in his eyes in the rear-view mirror. I grinned. "There's more, you know."

"More?"

"Ronnie's entire house is powered by the same technology. She has a small version of the engine that runs the pump on her water well. She's never out of electricity and it's totally free to run."

"Let me guess. It plugs right into the existing wiring like a conventional generator would?"

Ronnie nodded her head. "Just the same as having a generator for your house, except without the diesel."

Craig let out a low whistle. "Add another industry to the list of those who'd go to great lengths to stop Ronnie Oakhurst."

"Are you starting to see the big picture?" I asked.

Craig changed lanes to pass a string of cars. "I'm convinced. Independence from oil and power companies? Who wouldn't jump on that bandwagon? People would be knocking her doors down to get their hands on the engine. Can you imagine? Oil companies wouldn't have the power to manipulate people's lives. Gas prices wouldn't matter. High transportation costs wouldn't raise the price of everything people buy. People wouldn't have to worry if they'd be able to heat their homes in the winter, or cool them in the summer."

All those thoughts had gone through my head already. "How do you fight a power like that?"

"Quietly," Craig answered.

Ronnie stared out the window into the darkness. "I

should never have filed the patent. They'd never even know about it if I had kept it to myself."

"I'm surprised nobody has tried to buy your patent. I thought that's what usually happened when someone came up with an idea that threatened the big industries. Make a rich man out of the inventor and bury the idea so deep it won't stand a chance of seeing daylight," I said.

Ronnie turned around in her seat. "Someone did call me a few weeks ago. He said he was from a small manufacturing company up in L.A. He wanted to know more about the engine and if I'd consider a partnership. When I said no, he asked if I'd consider selling the patent. He didn't have a lot of financial backing and couldn't offer a big price. He didn't seem too upset when I told him no. We chatted for a while. Somehow, he knew about my father's inventions and asked if I was Melvin Oakhurst's daughter."

Ronnie pointed out the window at an upcoming street sign. "You want to make a left there," she told Craig.

"Anyhow, I never heard from him again."

"Doesn't sound like anyone from an oil company," I said.

"No, it doesn't," Craig said.

Ronnie pointed to another street sign. "Make a right there. I'm just about a half mile down on the left."

As we rounded the corner, a dozen flashing red lights caught our attention. As we got closer, we could see they were fire trucks.

"What's going on?" Ronnie blurted, staring at the fleet of big red trucks.

"Oh my God," I said as we rolled to a stop in front of what used to be Ronnie's house. All that remained was a pile of burning embers and a few charred two-by-fours left standing.

Chapter Five

The firemen at the scene told us the neighbors reported an explosion at Ronnie's house, followed by the fire that engulfed it within a matter of minutes.

Ronnie stood, dazed, in her driveway, watching the last of the embers turn black with the stream of water from the fire hoses. Craig and I gave her a few minutes to be alone, then we gradually coaxed her back to the car so we could take her back to our house.

The drive back to Del Mar seemed endless. I finally broke the silence. "You have insurance to rebuild, right?"

Ronnie sniffed. "Yes. That won't be a problem." The tears started flowing again. "It's not the house that I'm crying about. It's everything that was inside the house. All the memories. My projects. The model train—that took me forever to build. The pictures. All those pictures of my mom and dad and Lance and me—I can never get those back."

Craig drummed his thumbs on the steering wheel. "Any idea what might have caused the explosion? Did you use any flammable materials in your projects?" he asked.

"No. I didn't even keep a gas can around. Anything like that I kept out in the shop. Nothing in that house was prone to explode."

"No methane experiments? Anything like that?" Craig pressed.

"No. Why would I be experimenting with fuels? I have no reason to."

"I don't know. I just had to ask. I was hoping there'd be some logical explanation. If there's not, then I suspect someone destroyed your house on purpose," Craig said.

When we arrived home, I called Detective Wright to see if he'd had any luck locating Lance Oakhurst. He hadn't found him yet.

Ronnie sat on the floor in the corner of the living room, tears streaming down her face as she stroked the puppy's ears. He'd fallen asleep in her lap, thankful that someone finally came to his rescue and let him out of his new prison.

When I finally hung up the phone with Sam, after listening to his ten minute lecture about disobeying his orders by going to Ronnie's house, I sat down on the floor next to her.

"I know it doesn't seem like it right now, but everything's going to be okay," I said. How could I tell her such a thing? I had doubts that her life would ever be the same again. If our theory was right about the powers that might be after her, she'd never be safe.

Ronnie nodded her head and continued petting the puppy.

"Where did you put the folder you brought back from

your house? The one with the copies of the patents?" I asked.

Ronnie raised her chin and nodded toward the kitchen. "They're on the table. I was showing Craig the drawings for the engine before we left tonight."

I retrieved the folder from the kitchen and returned to our spot on the floor in the corner. I opened the folder and began taking out one page at a time. There were half a dozen copies of patents for different engines—some similar to Ronnie's, but not nearly as advanced. Some were for other types of engines—steam and fuel cell. I noted the applicant names. "They don't put the phone numbers on these?" I asked.

"No. Just the names of the patent holders and the cities where they live."

I reached over and stroked the puppy's ears. "He's really tired. You must be too. Why don't you go to bed? Tomorrow you can call your insurance company and get that whole process started."

Ronnie forced a smile and lifted the huge puppy, handing him to me. "Good idea. I'll see you in the morning."

I took the puppy out for one more potty check, then powered up the PC in my office. I logged onto the Internet and searched for telephone numbers or addresses to go with the names on the patents from Ronnie's file. Out of six names, the only two I could find phone numbers for were both on the East Coast. It was too late to try to call them. I decided to wait till morning.

Of the other four names, two were in southern California, not too far away. One was in Riverside and the other in Burbank. I couldn't get an address for the Burbank name, but I was able to find one for the Riverside name. The remaining two were in Nevada and Texas.

* * *

The next morning, I got up early to see Craig off to work. Ronnie was still asleep. I took the cordless phone to the kitchen table and unfolded the paper I'd written the phone numbers on the night before. The first name on the list was Casper Harris. I dialed the number, rehearsing what I was going to say when he answered. That never happened. I got a recording informing me that the number had been disconnected. I tried again, just in case I'd mis-dialed. Same recording. I made a note next to his name.

I dialed the second number and a woman answered on the third ring. "Hello?" she blurted into the phone, sounding out of breath.

"Hello. Is Ozie Dartmond in?" I asked.

"Mr. Dartmond? Oh, no," she replied, with a heavy Latino accent.

"Can you tell me when he might be home so I can call back?"

"He no coming home. He gone almost a year," she explained, in broken English.

I tapped my pencil on the table. "Gone? Has he moved?"

"Yes. He gone. Missis Dartmond throw him out," she said, sounding almost anxious to tell all the sordid details.

"I see. Do you have a number where I can reach him?"

"No. No number. He live somewhere in the Bahamas, I think. He sends child support and alimony check to Missis Dartmond, but they no speak. He not tell her how to find him. She happy as long as she gets money."

"Bahamas? Are you sure?"

"I pretty sure. Yes."

"I see. Well, thank you anyway," I said before I hung up the phone.

Bahamas. Isn't that where really rich people move to

avoid paying income taxes? I wondered if one of Ozie's inventions had paid off and put him in a new tax bracket.

The next name on the list was Clyde Waterman, who lived somewhere in Burbank. I had no address or phone number for him. I called the power company and waited for an answer.

"Hello. My name is Marcia Swenson. I'm the new bookkeeper for Clyde Waterman. He hasn't received his bill this month and I wanted to verify that you've sent it," I said.

The woman on the other end coughed into the receiver and cleared her throat. "What's the name again?"

"Marcia Swen—"

"Not your name, honey. The customer's name. Your name doesn't mean anything."

"Right. Clyde Waterman. He lives in Burbank."

I could hear her fingernails tapping computer keys. "You don't have his account number handy, do you?" she asked.

"No," I said.

"Of course you don't. Let's see. Yes, we mailed that out on the fifteenth. He should have it by now."

"Hmm. Well, he doesn't. Can you verify the address for me?"

"Sure, honey. What address do you have?" she asked. I could see this wasn't going to be easy.

I shuffled some papers on the table. "Let's see. He wrote it down for me, somewhere. Ah, here it is, I think. Five twenty-six Elm Street," I said. Every town has an Elm Street, doesn't it?

She chuckled. "Well, honey, that's not the address we have for Mr. Waterman. If he's expecting to get mail there, it's no wonder he hasn't received his bill."

"Can you tell me what address you did send it to?"

She ignored my question. "In fact, not only did we send

the bill out, but it's already been paid. Are you sure you're his bookkeeper?"

I cringed. "We must have had a miscommunication," I said, trying to think of some other way to get his address.

"In fact, as I read further, the bill was paid by Mr. Waterman's estate. It was the final payment on his account. Service has been stopped. It appears Mr. Waterman is deceased. So, how exactly *did* you communicate with him? A séance?"

"Deceased? When?" I asked.

"Honey, you better call someone else to get information. I got calls backed up ten deep. Every one of them waiting to chew me up one side and down the other because their electric bills have doubled, as if it were all my fault."

I hung up the phone. Deceased. I wondered what the cause of death was.

The next name on my list was Harvey Brewster. I had his address in Riverside but no telephone number. He was unlisted.

Ronnie shuffled into the kitchen, rubbing her puffy eyes and yawning. It didn't appear that she'd slept well.

"Good morning. Breakfast?" I asked.

"Oh, don't go to any trouble for me. I can just grab a piece of toast or something."

"It's no trouble. I scrambled some eggs for Craig. There's still some in the pan. Toast takes a second. Juice is in the fridge."

"Sounds great. Thanks," she said.

While Ronnie ate her eggs, I sat across the table from her. "After you talk to your insurance company, you feel like taking a drive with me? To Riverside?"

"Riverside? What's there?" she asked.

"Harvey Brewster. He filed a patent for—"

"I know the name. Why go see him?"

"Just talk to him. See if anyone has tried to buy his patent."

Ronnie nodded. "Okay."

I poured myself a glass of grapefruit juice. "Clyde Waterman is dead," I said.

"What? The fuel cell guy? When?"

"Not long ago. They just stopped his electric service this month."

"How'd he die?" she asked, sounding afraid of the answer.

"I don't know. I thought we could stop at the library first and go through the obituaries."

"You've been busy this morning. Anything else I should know about my peers?"

"Ozie Dartmond is living the good life somewhere in the Bahamas. Casper Harris's phone has been disconnected."

Ronnie frowned. "And the others?"

"I haven't gotten that far yet." I handed her the cordless phone. "You can use this to call your insurance company. Let me know when you're ready to go."

Clyde Waterman died after being struck by a hit-and-run driver. He was crossing the street in front of his house to collect his mail. It was nine in the morning. Visibility was good. There were no witnesses. There were no suspects. It happened only six weeks ago. Waterman lived alone and left behind no family. Ronnie chewed her bottom lip as she read the newspaper account. I gathered up my purse and stood. "Come on. Let's go," I said.

Ronnie navigated while I drove to Riverside. At her insistence, we took her car. She read the map and directed me around the streets in Riverside until we reached the street I'd written down. "What house number are we looking for?" I asked.

"Two forty-nine."

I checked the numbers on my side. They were even. "Okay, it'll be on your side."

We drove the entire block, but couldn't find the number. We found 243 and 255, but no 249. "I must have written it down wrong, or it was listed wrong. Let's stop and ask," I said, pulling to the curb in front of 243.

We walked to the front door and rang the bell. An old woman answered. I guessed her to be in her mid to late 80's. Her white hair was pulled back in a tight bun. She wore a brightly colored polka dotted dress that covered her legs to just below the knee. A pair of knee-high support hose were rolled down to her puffy ankles. I smiled at the blue Eeyore slippers she wore. "Hi. We're looking for this address," I said, showing her the slip of paper with Harvey Brewster's name and address. "We can't seem to find it. Do you happen to know where two forty-nine is?"

She studied the piece of paper. "Two forty-nine? That's Harvey's address."

I smiled. At least she knew him. Finally, we were getting somewhere.

"Yes. Is it close?" I asked.

"It's next door," she said.

"Next door? So he lives at two fifty-five?"

"No. Two forty-nine," she insisted.

"But there is no two forty-nine," I said.

"Not anymore. Burned to the ground, must be two years ago, I'd say."

I thought Ronnie was going to faint. I caught her arm and held her steady.

"Oh dear. Is she okay?" the old woman asked.

"She'll be fine. She's just a little—surprised. Do you know where Mr. Brewster lives now?" I asked.

"Oh, he doesn't. He was in the house when it went up. Bad gas leak or something. Blew to smithereens in the middle of the night. Poor man never knew what hit him."

Chapter Six

Gladys Dixon had lived at 243 Magnolia Street for the past 50 years. She invited us into her little house and offered Ronnie a chair to sit in before she fell down. I sat on the flower-print sofa and glanced around the tiny living room.

"Did you know Harvey well?" I asked.

Gladys picked a piece of lint from the arm of the over-stuffed chair she sat in. "Oh, probably as well as anyone could ever know Harvey. He was sort of a loner."

"Really? How long were you neighbors?" I asked.

Gladys pursed her lips and stared at the ceiling, calculating what appeared to be infinity in her head. "Let's see. He moved in next door right after Shelly was born. Shelly's my granddaughter. She just had her thirtieth birthday last week."

"Thirty years. That's a long time. Was he married?" I asked.

"Harvey? No. Never seemed interested in anything like that. Just wanted to tinker with all his little inventions. You knew he was an inventor?"

"Yes. Did he ever show them to you?"

"Oh, sure. He was as proud of those as a man would be about his own children. He'd come over sometimes late in the evening, banging on my door. 'Gladys!' he'd holler. 'Come see what I've made!' he'd yell through the window, excited as a kid with a new toy."

Ronnie smiled, apparently able to identify with Harvey's excitement. "Do you remember him showing you an engine he designed?" Ronnie asked.

"The steam engine?" Gladys prompted.

"That's the one," Ronnie said.

"Oh, sure. He said it was his greatest invention so far. It was going to change the world."

I noticed a collection of photos on the wall behind Gladys. One caught my attention. It was of a younger Gladys sitting in the passenger seat of a bright orange dune buggy with the words, *Brewster's Steamer*, painted on the side. The man in the driver's seat had a smile spread across his face so wide I could barely see his ears for his cheeks. "Is that Harvey?" I asked, pointing toward the picture. Gladys turned in her chair to see.

"That's him. What fun we had. He'd drive me down to the grocery store whenever I needed something. Nice fellow, he was. They took my driver's license away a few years back, when I couldn't pass the test anymore. That's *Brewster's Steamer* we're in, there. I think that picture was taken before he added the heating gizmo."

"Heating gizmo?" I asked.

"Yeah. He had some big fancy name for it. I could never remember. All I know is it could get really hot—hot enough to make steam, and it could do it without kerosene, like his first engine needed."

"Really?" Ronnie asked. I could hear the anticipation in her voice as she formed her next question. "What kind of fuel did it use?"

"According to Harvey, it didn't use any fuel. All that technical mumbo-jumbo talk went right over my head. He tried to explain it to me fifty times or more, but I told him it was no use. All I cared about was that it got me to the store and back so I could make banana bread with walnuts and raisins. That man did love my banana bread."

Ronnie and I exchanged glances. Another engine that was apparently free to run, and the inventor killed in a freak explosion. We thanked Gladys for the information and left her to finish whatever chores we'd interrupted.

"Do you know how much horsepower can be generated from steam?" she asked, testing my knowledge.

"No, but I bet you're going to tell me," I replied. I started the car and pulled away from the curb.

"A lot," she said.

"A lot? That's your answer?"

"You know how much a train weighs?" she continued.

"Let me guess. A lot?"

"Yes. A lot. And for years, steam was how we powered those old locomotives. Unbelievable horsepower. And to be able to generate the kind of heat you need to create steam without using fuel is an enormous breakthrough. If Harvey had what Gladys is describing—"

"Then it probably wasn't an accident that his house blew up," I said.

Ronnie sunk down in her seat. She chewed on her thumbnail as she stared out the window.

"I think we should talk to Jake Monroe," I said.

Ronnie looked at me, surprised. "Jake? Believe me, he's not involved with any of this."

I wondered how she could be so sure. "It just seems strange that he'd encourage you to file your patent, after what you told us about him."

I sat across from Ronnie at our kitchen table as she dialed Jake Monroe's number in Detroit. "He might be back by now. His message the other night said he'd be out of town for a few days," she said as she waited for someone to answer the phone. I would liked to have been on another extension so I could listen to the entire conversation, but I settled for just the one side I'd be able to hear from Ronnie.

"Jake Monroe, please," she requested.

I watched her impatiently tap her fingers on the table. When she stopped tapping, I knew he'd picked up the phone. "Jake, it's Ronnie." There was a brief pause. "I know. No. I didn't go to Cabo." Another pause. "I'm fine— no, I'm not fine. Someone tried to kill me. They blew up my house."

I could hear Jake Monroe's voice over the phone. "What?" He sounded extremely alarmed.

"I said someone tried to kill me. I'm pretty sure it has something to do with my engine." Ronnie listened to him for nearly a full minute. "There are others—two that I know of so far—who've been killed after they filed for patents on their engines."

Ronnie listened again, then rolled her eyes. "I'm not imagining it, Jake. These guys came up with ideas that were way ahead of their time. Now they're dead. I'm afraid I'm going to be next." Her hand began shaking. The tone of voice she used with Jake led me to wonder if they were more than just business acquaintances. I detected the subtle combination of irritation and affection.

"I want to know why you told me to file the patent. Do you have any plans to use the engine?" Ronnie asked.

"Then why?" she demanded.

"No, I'm not blaming you, but—

"I'm staying with friends.

"At this point, I don't trust anyone.

"No, I haven't forgotten the last time."

Ronnie's voice turned to a whisper. She turned around in her chair to try to make the conversation private. "I can't discuss that with you right now."

She cleared her throat and turned to face me again. "Do you have any idea who might be behind this?" she asked, bringing the conversation back to center.

"No. I didn't think so. Well, thanks for all your help, Jake," she delivered with a sarcasm I hadn't heard from her before. She hung up the phone.

I flashed her a sympathetic look. "No help?" I asked.

"I don't understand that man," she said, frustration ringing in her voice. "He'll sit in a meeting with his team of engineers and pass on every proposal that shows any promise of hitting one out of the park in favor of the ones that merely meet some insignificant government requirement. Then he'll turn around and curse the oil companies for holding the world hostage by demanding ransom at the fuel pump."

"It sounds like he's torn—fighting some war waged in his own conscience," I said.

I slid Ronnie's folder across the table toward me and flipped it open. I spread the six patents out in front of me. Harvey Brewster and Clyde Waterman were dead. Ozie

Dartmond was living it up in the Bahamas. Casper Harris was a big question mark. His phone had been disconnected.

"We need to find out what's going on with these other two guys—Gus Tiller and Bo Rawlings. I couldn't find anything on them on the Internet," I said. I noticed a name and address at the top of Gus Tiller's patent paperwork. "Who's this?" I asked.

She looked at the name. "That would be the patent attorney who did the actual filing."

The address was in Boulder, Colorado. A patent attorney was also listed on Bo Rawlings' paperwork. I called information and got both phone numbers in less than a minute.

Bo Rawlings' attorney was not very helpful. "Client confidentiality" was his favorite phrase. He would not give me an address or phone number for Bo. I gave him my name and number and asked if he would relay it to Bo and have him contact me. The matter was urgent, I told him. He did allow one interesting piece of information to slip when he told me that Bo and his family lived outside the continental United States in a time zone that made it difficult to contact him at the moment. I assumed that meant Alaska or Hawaii, or maybe even Puerto Rico.

Gus Tiller's attorney was not in, but his secretary had no qualms about discussing Gus. Client confidentiality didn't seem to be part of her vocabulary. I suppose it was because all the details she'd spilled to me had been reported in the local newspapers at the time the events took place. Gus disappeared from his studio apartment six years ago. He'd been missing for over a year when a pair of brothers, who were out riding their motorcycles in the desert, found his body—well, one part, anyway. Wild animals had probably carried off the rest of Gus, but they left his head. Dental records confirmed his identity.

I asked what would happen to Gus's patent since he was dead. She explained that the patent was only good for seventeen years, subject, of course, to additional maintenance fees. Since there were no heirs or other family members to keep up the fees, the patent would be considered abandoned.

I thanked her for the information and hung up the phone.

Ronnie studied my face. She looked as concerned as I felt. I slid Gus Tiller's patent across the table to the side reserved for the dead inventors.

Craig walked in and dropped his keys on the counter. He crossed the kitchen and kissed me on top of the head. "Honey, I'm home," he said, then smiled as though he'd just had a thought. "I've always wanted to say that."

I smiled back. "Hi, honey. How was your day?"

"Oh, you know, the same old same old. One tonsillectomy, an emergency appendectomy, and a sixty-eight-year-old who broke her arm while in-line skating with her eleven-year-old grandson."

"Ouch," I said.

"How was your day?" he asked, taking the chair next to mine and studying the papers spread out on the table.

"We tracked down five of the six guys from Ronnie's patent search file. Well, four actually. Bo Rawlings is alive and living in another time zone. If I had to guess, I'd say he's living well off of revenue from the sale of his patent. I guess we could hire our own attorney and find out who owns his patent now." I motioned toward the separate sections on the table. "Three dead, one alive and rich, one alive and questionable, but probably rich, and one unknown," I said. "The question is, how does someone get to be in the 'rich inventor club' instead of the 'dead inventor' one?"

"What do the dead ones have in common? What do the rich ones have in common?" Craig asked.

I looked to Ronnie for a suggestion. "Were the dead ones' inventions more threatening to the oil companies?" I asked.

Ronnie shook her head. "There doesn't seem to be a pattern there. Ozie Dartmond's idea would have been the most damaging to the oil industry, and he's alive and well. Harvey Brewster's held equally as much potential, yet he's dead. I don't get it."

Craig shook his head. "Hmm. This is a tough one. What else do we know about them?"

We all stared at the papers spread out in front of us. Then Craig broke the silence. "Where's the puppy?"

"You mean our son?" I asked, joking.

"Yeah. Where's my boy?"

"He's out back playing with the new puppy toys I bought him."

"Does he have a name yet?" Craig asked.

"Not yet," I confessed, ashamed that I hadn't even thought about puppy names the entire day. Then it struck me. "Wait! That's it!" I blurted.

"What?" Ronnie asked.

"What if it has to do with leverage?" I continued.

"Leverage?" Craig asked.

"Yes. Pressure. It's easy to force someone to do something they don't want to do if you have enough leverage on them."

Ronnie followed my thinking. "Family," she said.

"Exactly. Harvey Brewster—no family—dead. Clyde Waterman—no family—dead. Gus Tiller—no family—dead. On the other hand, Bo Rawlings—happy family—alive and well. Ozie Dartmond—ex-wife and children, granted, not the traditional happy family, but still, blood relatives—living it up in the Bahamas," I said.

Craig nodded. "Makes sense. So you think whoever is behind this put pressure on these two to sell their patents, threatening their families if they didn't cooperate?"

"That's got to be it. But where does that leave Ronnie? No one has made her any offers," I said.

"Don't forget the guy from L.A." Craig reminded me.

"I mean a real offer. And there was no threat. They just tried to send her directly to the 'dead inventor club' without offering her membership in the 'live rich' one."

"That reminds me. Has Sam found Lance yet?" Craig asked.

Ronnie frowned. "Not yet. He should have been back this morning. What if they've done something to him?"

"They wouldn't have any reason to hurt him. He doesn't take after your father the same way you do, does he?" I asked.

"How do you mean?" Ronnie asked.

"Is he also an inventor?"

"No. Lance races cars—period."

"Then they'd have no reason to hurt him unless they'd made some threat to you. It wouldn't do them any good to hurt him if they didn't first give you a chance to deal with them," I assured her.

"I guess you're right, but I'm still worried about him."

"He's only a day late. Maybe they're having such a good time, they decided to stay a little longer," I offered. I put as much sincerity in the suggestion as I could, but I had a feeling it wasn't enough. The worry didn't leave Ronnie's face.

"Do you have any other family? Anyone especially close to you?" I asked.

Ronnie shook her head. "Lance is all I have." Then the tears started flowing down her cheeks.

The phone rang and nearly startled me out of my seat. I picked it up and pressed the TALK button.

"Hello?"

"Devonie. It's Sam," he said.

I smiled and gave Ronnie a relieved look. I was sure he was calling to tell me they'd found Lance and the rest of the crew. "Hi Sam. You have good news for us?" I asked.

"Not really."

I turned away from the table. "What's up?" I said, trying to not sound overly concerned, for Ronnie's sake. "Did you find Lance?" I continued.

"Not exactly."

I waited. "What do you mean, not exactly?"

"We found the boat—*The Dream Catcher*—but it was abandoned. No one on board," he explained.

"Abandoned? Where?"

By this time, Ronnie was on her feet and moved to face me. I couldn't hide my expression from her. She grew pale.

"Just adrift, near a marina in Cabo San Lucas."

I tried to maintain calmness in my voice. "Are you looking for them?"

"We don't have jurisdiction down there, but the Mexican police assure us they're doing everything possible to locate the crew."

"What do you think happened?" I asked.

"I don't know. There wasn't anything wrong with the boat, so it's not likely they took up with another boat to get help. Could've been pirates. 'Low-key' is the last word I'd use to describe *The Dream Catcher*. Everything about it says the people on board have money."

"But if it were pirates, they wouldn't have left the boat. It's too valuable," I speculated.

"Depends on what they're after. The boat would be tough to disguise. Maybe they just wanted the valuables of the people on board—much easier to turn into cash. But that doesn't explain why the people on board were missing—unless . . ."

"Unless?" I pressed.

"Unless they didn't want to leave witnesses. Then again, if they're after ransom, they'd leave the boat for effect— you know, get the attention of the families."

I cringed. Ransom. What a scary word. But better than dead witnesses. At least if they were kidnapped, there'd be a chance to get them back alive. "So what do we do now?"

"We wait," Sam replied.

"Wait? You're thinking ransom demand?"

"Maybe. We have to see what happens next."

"Sam, what if nothing happens? What if no one calls?"

"Something always happens, Devonie. You can count on it."

I hung up the phone and motioned for Ronnie to sit down. Somehow, I'd have to relay to her the conversation I'd just had with Sam and still remain hopeful that she'd get her brother back—alive.

Chapter Seven

"How far is it to Cabo?" Ronnie asked.

I squeezed my eyes shut and tried to calculate the miles. "About—"

"Now, wait a minute," Craig interrupted. "We're not going to Cabo."

"But we already know the police aren't doing anything," Ronnie argued.

"They didn't say that. They don't have jurisdiction, but the Mexican police are working on it," Craig reminded her.

Ronnie and I rolled our eyes.

"How much bribe money do you suppose it would take to get them to actually lift a finger to find Lance?" Ronnie asked sarcastically.

Craig didn't have an answer. He knew she was probably right. "Let's just say, for argument's sake, that we go to Cabo. What do we do when we get there? We aren't detectives. We don't speak the language—"

"I do," Ronnie said.

Craig looked at me. "Why does that not surprise me?" he said.

I smiled at him. "I bet she's fluent, too."

Ronnie nodded. "I speak seven languages. It's sort of a hobby."

Craig shook his head. "Okay, so one of us speaks the language. That doesn't necessarily make us good candidates. It could be dangerous."

Ronnie laid her hands, palms down, on the table. "I don't expect you to come with me. I know it's risky. I don't want to get anyone hurt."

"Yeah, right. I'm not going to let you go by yourself," I said.

"Wait a minute," Craig jumped in. "I'm not letting either one of you go."

I raised my eyebrows and gave him the "you're my husband not my father" look.

He rephrased. "Use your head. If you want to find Lance, hire a professional. Get a private investigator—someone with experience. We go down there and it'll be 'The Three Stooges'—a regular circus."

I looked at Ronnie. "That's not a bad idea. What do you think?"

Craig let out a sigh of relief. Finally, we were being rational.

Ronnie nodded. "I guess it makes sense, but how do I find someone who'll do it?"

I searched Craig's face. "Do you know anyone?" I asked.

"He shook his head. "No, but I bet Sam can recommend someone."

"Good idea. I'll give him a call."

* * *

Rick Caper and Gary Lawless, the partners who make up Caper and Lawless Investigations, kept a small office in downtown San Diego. I chuckled when I read the sign and wondered if those were their real names or if they chose them for effect. Sam gave me a brief rundown on the pair. When they weren't working on a case, they were stuntmen for the movie studios. They specialized in car chases, car crashes, and motorcycle stunts. Sam met them when they were working as stuntmen on a popular television series about California Highway Patrolmen. The studio allowed them freedom to use the police motorcycles off the set. The pair thought it would be great fun to race down the Hollywood Freeway in uniform on the motorcycles, popping wheelies to entertain the commuters. Needless to say, the highway patrol received so many complaints that the studio had to revoke their costume and motorcycle privileges off the set.

Rick stood 6' 2", easily, with thick black hair and a mustache just beginning to show a hint of gray. He wore Levis, Nike high-tops, and a T-shirt with the words *No Fear* printed across the front. I imagine that's a job requirement in his line of work.

Gary stood equally as tall, but had blond hair and was clean-shaven. I guessed his age to be around the same as Rick's—mid- to late-forties. A pair of Ray-Ban sunglasses hung from a string around his neck. When he turned to lead us into their office, I had to laugh at the words printed on the back of his T-shirt: *Official Bomb Technician—If you see me running, try to keep up.*

Ronnie and I sat across from Rick and Gary in their small office. Ronnie explained the situation with Lance in great detail. While she talked, I noticed photos of Rick and Gary on the walls, mugging for the camera, with several high-profile stars. I recognized Al Pacino, Clint Eastwood, Tom Cruise, Mel Gibson, Tom Selleck, and Sam Elliot.

Gary took notes while Ronnie told her story. When she finished, Rick stood and asked, "Can I get you something to drink? Soda? Beer?"

I shook my head. "No, thanks."

Ronnie asked for a Coke.

Rick returned from some other room with a soda for Ronnie and two longneck bottles from some local brewery I didn't recognize.

"Thanks, Rick," Gary said, taking one of the bottles.

Out of reflex, I checked my watch, noticing the time was way before noon. Gary noticed my movement and smiled.

"It's root beer," he explained. "We don't break out the hard stuff till after lunch."

I smiled and nodded.

Rick reclaimed his seat and twisted the top off his bottle. "What d'ya think?" he asked Gary.

"I think these ladies came to the right place," Gary said, grinning.

Rick nodded. "You thinking what I'm thinking?"

Gray's grin grew to expose nearly every tooth in his mouth. "I don't know. Are you thinking we load up the dirt bikes on the trailer and head to Baja? We pose as a couple of riders looking for their good buddy, the famous NASCAR driver, Lance Oakhurst?"

Rick shook his head. "I was thinking we load up our fishing gear and head to Cabo. Looking for our fishing buddy, Lance Oakhurst."

Gary gave a moment of thought to Rick's suggestion, then nodded his head.

"But your idea works, too," Rick offered.

I observed the team working on their game plan. "Is there some reason you can't do both?" I asked.

"I like the way you think," Gary said, pointing a finger at me.

Somehow, I got the feeling this would be more fun than work for Rick and Gary, but if the result was that they found Lance, then it didn't matter to me if they brought along a whole amusement park.

"Can you get us pictures of all the people who went on the trip?" Rick asked.

Ronnie frowned. "All my pictures were destroyed in the fire."

"What about Lance? He must keep pictures," I said.

Ronnie nodded. "He does. And I have a key to his house. I'm just not sure where he keeps them. We'll have to do a little hunting."

"Great," Rick said. "I'll call Sam and get everything he found out from the Mexican police."

Gary opened a date planner and studied the pages. "We have to be back here in a week for the shoot in San Francisco."

"The Russell Crowe thing?" Rick asked.

"No, that's the following week. This is the Bruce Willis movie. Remember?"

"Right. We could leave tomorrow. That'd give us a few days."

Ronnie and I met Rick and Gary in front of their office at seven the next morning. A big white pickup truck was parked at the curb. A trailer with two motorcycles perched on it, tied down with nylon straps, was hitched to the truck.

While Rick collected the photos from Ronnie, I watched Gary make a last-minute check of the gear they'd stowed in the back of the pickup, protected by a camper shell. I saw helmets, leathers, sleeping bags, fishing gear, ice chests—all the paraphernalia a couple of dirt bike buddies would take along on a fishing/riding expedition. Gary jumped out over the tailgate, closed the camper shell down tight and locked it.

"We ready to roll?" Gary called to Rick.

"I think so. You get a number for us so we can call in reports?"

"Got it right here," Gary said, as he patted his pocket. I'd given him a slip of paper with all the phone numbers I could think of to reach Ronnie, Craig, or myself.

"Then let's hit it. Baja, here we come."

I watched the team of Caper and Lawless drive away with their truck and trailer load of "tools," and said a little prayer that they'd be successful in finding Lance Oakhurst and his crew, alive and well.

Ronnie and I climbed back into my Explorer. She slammed her door shut and looked at me. "Now what?"

I gave her a blank stare.

"I can't just sit around and wait. I have to do something," she insisted.

"Okay. I'd say there's plenty we can do from here. First on our list is to find out who's trying to kill you. I think it's kind of interesting that the guy who wanted to buy your patent knew about your father. How much do you remember about the time he was killed?"

Ronnie frowned. I was heading into painful territory. "Not much. I was pretty little."

"Is there anyone who knew about your father's engine? Someone who might remember connections your father may have made around the time of his death?"

Ronnie searched her memory. "Dad used to go to a little

machine shop not far from where we lived—Harold's shop. We'd gone there that day—the day of the explosion—to weld something. Dad and Harold were good friends."

"Do you know where Harold is now?" I asked.

"Oh, Harold was old back then. He's dead by now."

Disappointment showed on my face.

"But Larry's still around," Ronnie offered.

"Larry?"

"He worked for Harold. He's still around. He and his son have a shop in Escondido. They have a CNC mill. I have them machine parts for me once in a while."

"CNC?" I questioned.

"It's a computerized milling machine. It can make just about anything you can imagine. It's a cool piece of equipment."

"Did Larry know your dad well?"

"I don't think so, but he knew about the fuel cell engine. He and Harold were pretty tight. I'm sure Harold told him all about my dad."

"Then I'd say we should go talk to Larry."

I followed Ronnie through the maze of machines, cars, motorcycles, and racks full of various shapes and sizes of sheet metal and rods. We walked past what must have been the office. A large window allowed a view into the semi-organized room. I noticed an assortment of framed photos hanging on the walls. I stopped momentarily to study them. By the looks of the cars in the pictures, they must have dated all the way back to the 1950's. A few were from the 1960's. As my eyes advanced along the wall, I deduced that they were organized chronologically, with the most recent disappearing around a corner, out of my view. I didn't recognize any of the faces in the photos, but the general theme was very similar to the photos I'd observed at Ronnie's house—man's infatuation with machines. Cars, motorcycles, boats, planes. A couple of the pictures seemed a little out of place. They were more human interest rather than mechanical. I guess that's why they caught my attention. I suddenly realized Ronnie had left me behind, so I scurried through the shop to catch up with her.

A tall, slender man with curly gray hair glanced over his big safety glasses at us and smiled. "Hey, Ronnie. What brings you out here?"

"Hi Larry," Ronnie replied. "I've come to see if I can buy you lunch."

"Lunch? You need a favor? Something machined right away?"

Ronnie laughed. "Not today." She motioned toward me. "This is my friend, Devonie. We wondered if you could talk to us about my dad . . . you know . . . the explosion?"

Larry smiled at me, then returned a confused look to Ronnie. "Your dad? I don't know what I can tell you."

"Anything you can remember, Larry. It's really important," Ronnie pleaded.

Larry seemed to sense the desperation in her voice. "Okay, kid. Just let me set up this run. I got an order for twenty jacks. They gotta go out tomorrow."

I watched Larry bolt a sheet of metal to a plate inside a large box with windows on two sides. He closed a door on the machine, slipped a floppy disk into a drive, and punched some buttons. Cutting bits started spinning and arms and levers began moving inside the box. Slowly, a shape was cut out of the metal, and then another. Larry watched, satisfied that the program was running smoothly.

"Once in a while, it'll get a wild hair and cut out twenty parts with a big ol' hole smack dab in the middle. Ruin a whole sheet," Larry explained. "Looks okay, though. You ready? Let's go."

Larry ordered a steak. Ronnie and I ordered salads. While we waited for our lunches, Ronnie told Larry about the attempt on her life, the burning of her house, and Lance's disappearance. Larry appeared shocked.

"Egads. Are the police doing anything?" he asked.

Ronnie shook her head. "They're doing what they can, I guess, but I'm afraid it's not going to be enough. Do you remember the fuel cell engine my dad was working on when he died?"

Larry chuckled as he recalled the last time he'd seen Ronnie's father. "Thought he was gonna blow the whole place up the day he brought that tank in and started welding on it."

I sat forward in my seat. "Blow the place up? Was his engine prone to explode?" I asked, wondering if maybe Mel Oakhurst caused his own death.

"Turns out it wasn't. Harold explained it to me. He was using metal hydride. It's non-explosive."

"Do you think something Mel did caused the explosion?" I asked.

Larry cut a piece of steak and put it in his mouth. When he finished chewing, he started talking again. "Mel came over to our shop at least once a week to weld something. He wouldn't even keep an oxygen tank at his house. He didn't want to have anything around that might be danger-ous to his family. Never met anyone more worried about stuff like that. I guess that's part of the reason he decided to make the fuel cell engine. He was bent on saving the world from itself."

"So you don't think the explosion was an accident?" I asked.

Larry set his fork down. "There was a lot of talk back then, when it happened, you know. Mel was supposed to demo the engine for some potential investors. Talk was they were going to mass-produce it, if it performed as advertised. After the explosion, rumors were that the oil companies did it to protect their interests. No one could ever prove it. I think that's why they just called it an accident, so they could put it to rest."

Ronnie's face grimaced as though she'd just swallowed a bitter pill. "Put it to rest? It'll never be put to rest. They just keep killing the people who threaten their interests, or buying them off."

Larry looked at me, somewhat confused. "Did I miss something? What people are we talking about?"

"Since Mel's death, we've discovered a few more inventors who've died under questionable circumstances. Others sold their patents and are living the good life. We think the same person or people are probably behind all these killings. That's why we're here. Do you remember anything about any connections Mel may have made around the time he died?"

Larry scratched his head. "I don't recall. It was a long time ago. Harold did tell me the fellas who were interested in the engine were from some small manufacturing company up in L.A. Small-time outfit looking to hit it big. What was the name of that outfit? Had a funny name, I remember. Something like oyster or clam. Shell? Maybe. Gosh, I can't remember."

Ronnie sat forward in her seat. Her eyes grew wider. "Was it Pearle? Pearle Manufacturing?" she asked.

"That's it. Pearle. I knew it was something like that," Larry said, snapping his fingers.

Ronnie's face grew as pale as the paper napkin in my lap. "How do you know Pearle Manufacturing?" I asked her.

"Jack Pearle. That's the name of the guy from L.A. who wanted to partner with me on my engine. Pearle Manufacturing."

"The one who didn't have any money?"

"That's the one," she said.

We dropped Larry off at his shop and headed for the nearest library and a Los Angeles telephone directory. There was no Pearle Manufacturing listed in the entire county.

"Didn't the guy give you a number to call him—in case you changed your mind?" I asked Ronnie.

"He did, but I knew I wouldn't change my mind. I think I threw it away. Even if I'd kept it, it's gone now—burned to a crisp."

"Well, I think we've got another piece to this puzzle. Mighty big coincidence that this Jack Pearle would be interested in your dad's engine just before the big explosion—"

"Then he wants in on mine, and, *déjà vu*, another explosion."

The phone was ringing when we walked through the front door of our house. Craig still wasn't home from the hospital. I raced to the kitchen and picked it up, hoping I wasn't too late. "Hello?" I said, slightly out of breath.

The call was for Ronnie, from her insurance company. I handed her the phone and went to let the puppy in.

The puppy. Still no name for my poor little "son". I squeezed him and gave him a kiss on top of his head. "What are we going to name you? Hoss?"

He wagged his tail.

I gave him a doubtful look. "I don't think Craig will go for it. Not dignified enough."

I heard Ronnie's voice from the kitchen. "What?" she nearly screamed.

I ran to see what was wrong. She was barking into the telephone. "That's crazy! No way! It's a lie!" she yelled.

"What's wrong?" I mouthed.

She squeezed her eyes shut, fighting back tears. "Your guy is a liar," she blurted, then slammed the phone down on its cradle.

"What was that all about?" I asked.

Her face was nearly as red as her hair. I took her arm and led her to a chair, which she collapsed into. "They said they're not going to pay on my claim," she said, sobbing.

"What? Why?" I asked, dumbfounded.

"They . . . they said I had dangerous chemicals—that I was running some sort of meth lab. They threatened to report me to the police for manufacturing methamphetamine."

I gaped at her. "Where'd they get an idea like that?"

"They said the investigator from the fire department told them. He said that was the cause of the explosion and the fire. It's all a lie. A big lie," she insisted, wiping her eyes with the sleeve of her shirt.

I handed her a box of Kleenex. The puppy sat at Ronnie's feet and rested his head on her knee. He looked genuinely concerned for her, his brown eyes almost as teary as hers. At the moment, I couldn't offer any more comfort than he was providing. The doorbell rang, so I left her in the puppy's care while I answered the door.

The man standing on my front porch was tall—6' 4" at least, and handsome. Clark Gable was the first thought that flashed through my mind when I opened the door. His dark hair was cut short on the sides and back, but the extra length on top allowed the waves to fall across his forehead. His eyes were hazel or green—I couldn't tell for sure. I stood there, like the village idiot, waiting for him to recite his line: "Frankly Scarlett . . ."

He smiled at me. I think I might have blushed.

"Is Ronnie Oakhurst here?" he asked.

I managed to close my mouth before any bugs flew in, or anything stupid fell out of it.

He smiled again. "Ronnie Oakhurst? Is she here?" he repeated.

I shook my head as though I'd just been released from a deep trance. "Ronnie? Who's asking?"

"Tell her Jake is here. Jake Monroe."

Chapter Eight

Caller ID is how Jake Monroe found Ronnie. When she called him from our phone, Craig's name and telephone number appeared on a display on Jake's phone. From there, it was a simple matter of using a reverse phone directory to get the address.

Craig and I sat at the breakfast nook and watched through the bay window as Ronnie and Jake walked down the dock for a private talk. Jake opened the walk-through gate for her, then took her hand and held it as they continued to stroll.

"What do you see when you look at them?" I asked Craig.

He studied the pair for a moment. "I see a couple who appear to be in love."

"This is how I know you're definitely the more romantic of the two of us," I replied.

"Why? What do you see?" he asked.

"I see a woman who's invented an engine that's free to run. I see a man who's in a position to put that engine in every car World Motors builds. I see that they're more than just acquaintances. They're not trying to hide it."

"Meaning that we're not the only ones who know about their relationship," Craig added.

"If that happens—if Jake gets World Motors to tool up to build Ronnie's engine—it'll spread like a wildfire. It'll be the beginning of the end for oil companies."

"I'd say it's a miracle that Ronnie's still alive," Craig said.

"And probably the only reason Jake hasn't been eliminated is his willingness to honor the wishes of the oil companies that pull his strings. Ronnie said he basically does whatever they tell him."

Craig and I watched the couple stop at the end of the dock. Ronnie wrapped her arms around Jake's neck and he returned the gesture by holding her close and kissing her.

"If *that* picture doesn't scare the heck out of every oilman in the world, I don't know what would," I said.

Jake, Ronnie, Craig, and I sat around the dining room table eating the best meal I could prepare in less than thirty minutes—spaghetti with toasted garlic bread and a green salad. Craig poured red wine for all of us.

"So, Jake. How'd you and Ronnie meet?" I asked.

Jake and Ronnie exchanged glances, then they both laughed.

"We met last year at Daytona. My company had given me a pit pass. One of the perks of working for World Motors—I get to play on their dime. Anyhow, Lance was racing, so Ronnie was there, working on his car. I spotted her cute little . . . coveralls, buried halfway under the hood. Not too often you see a woman mechanic at the track. I was intrigued, so I introduced myself. Offered some advice on the timing—sounded a little off to me. Anyhow, she let me know that my advice was neither needed nor appreciated."

Ronnie shot him a defensive look. "I was nice to you."

"Like heck you were," he shot back. "If I had any less self-confidence, I'd have run away with my tail between my legs instead of hanging around to take more of your abuse."

"Abuse. You don't know abuse. You're just too sensitive," she joked.

Jake grinned at her. "So I hung around and pestered her until she finally told me she had to leave. She climbed into her souped-up golf cart and peeled out like she was driving one of those racecars she works on. The tires actually burned rubber on the pavement. I'd never seen anything like it."

I caught Ronnie's attention. "Your engine?" I asked.

She shook her head. "Not the same one that's in my car. I put a little steam engine in the cart. That one I showed you my plans for."

Jake continued. "I followed her to the team's trailer and begged her to tell me about the golf cart. I was fascinated and offered to buy her dinner if she'd show me her other engines."

Ronnie shook her finger at him. "Admit it. You were just interested in getting a date with me. You used the excuse of wanting to see the engines just to get on my good side."

"Guilty as charged," Jake admitted. "Anyhow, after the race was over, I bought her dinner. Somehow in the conversation about all her inventions, she told me where she lived. The next week, I flew to California, then I drove out to her place. She wheeled a funny-looking motorcycle out of her garage—looked like a little Yamaha two-fifty, but with an engine like I'd never seen before. She sat on the seat and told me to climb on behind her. Then she told me to hang on." Jake smiled and rolled his eyes. "Yeah, right. But the thing wasn't even running yet. I thought she was crazy. She told me, again, to hold on. I asked 'what for?' Then she spurred that thing on, and I fell right off the back. Knocked the wind out of me."

Craig chuckled at the thought. "No kidding? Had some kick, did it?"

"Kick? You can say that again. She literally knocked me off my feet."

We all laughed.

"But Ronnie said you live in Detroit. That's taking the term 'long distance relationship' to a new level," I said.

Jake smiled and nodded. "I've tried to convince her to leave the land of the short thermometer for Michigan. I just don't understand why she wouldn't want to move. I mean, once you get used to the ice storms and the sub-zero temperatures in the winter, and the heat and humidity in the summer, what's the problem?"

"Can you blame me?" Ronnie said. "I don't know why you don't move here."

Jake smiled at her. "Believe me, it's very tempting. For now, we have to do the tele-relationship thing and grab every weekend opportunity we can to get together. You know how demanding my job is. All the engines are in Detroit."

"Not *all* the engines," Ronnie reminded him.

I used this opportunity to bring up the subject. "So I take it you've got some interest in the engine Ronnie has in her car? The heat-exchange engine?"

Jake frowned. "It's a very interesting concept. It has a lot of potential."

Ronnie rolled her eyes. "It has more than potential. It could change the world."

"You don't understand. It's very complicated. You can't just upset the balance of nature, so to speak," Jake said.

"Oh, I understand," Ronnie said. "I understand that you're in the back pockets of the oil companies. I understand that they're a bunch of greedy vultures, picking meat off the bones of the working-class people who are struggling to make ends meet."

Craig and I sat back and watched this argument flare up. It was obviously a re-hashing of something that had been discussed over and over in the past.

"Ronnie, I've told you this a thousand times. The whole world's economy is a delicate balancing act. If you pull the legs out from under an industry as big as oil, it'd be like knocking the earth off its axis. You know how many people would be out of jobs? How many companies would go under? It'd be a disaster."

Ronnie gritted her teeth. "It wouldn't happen overnight, Jake. There'd be time to re-group. There'd still be jobs; they'd just be in a different industry. It's gonna happen anyway, and you know it. It's not just a matter of cost to the consumer, either. We can't continue to pump four hundred and sixty-nine million metric tons of carbon into the air every year and expect to be a healthy race of people."

Craig and I exchanged glances. I had no idea the number was so high, and I could tell by the surprise on his face that he didn't either.

Jake placed his palms over his eyes and shook his head. "Don't get started on the whole environmental thing again. Today's engines burn so much cleaner than they used to—"

"And there's so many more of them now, that the net effect is that the same amount of poison is released into the air. How many more people have to have some part of their body cut off because of a cancerous tumor before someone has the guts to stop this madness?"

"Don't start on the whole cancer thing."

"Don't start? When my mother was thirty, she couldn't name one personal acquaintance that either had or died of cancer. When I was thirty, I could name a dozen off the top of my head—and they were all under fifty."

"But that's only because we've gotten better at diagnosing cancer. She had to know people who died of something, but no one put the label 'cancer' on it because they didn't know it back then."

"Oh, come on, Jake. We're not talking about the middle ages, here. Pull your head out of the sand. You sound just like the fast-talking bull-sellers who continue to shovel that theory down our throats every chance they get. Like we're too stupid to see the facts for ourselves."

Jake was silent.

Ronnie was just getting started. "And at thirty-six, my mother died of lung cancer. She never smoked a day in her life. Explain that one to me, Mr. Monroe."

Craig reached across the table for the bottle of merlot. "More wine, anyone?"

I knew what Craig was thinking. Let's get some more alcohol in them to settle them down before they get into a knock-down drag-out brawl in the middle of the dining room.

Ronnie took in a short, quick breath and put her hand over her mouth. She was embarrassed. "I'm sorry. I shouldn't have started this argument in front of the two of you. I don't know what I was thinking. You must think I'm some kind of kook," she apologized.

Jake reached over the table and took her hand. "You're not a kook. You're just passionate. There's nothing wrong with that. In fact, that's the reason I'm so crazy about you."

I cleared my throat and tried to think of a tactful way to bring up the subject of their relationship. "Speaking of how crazy you are about her—how much of that is common knowledge?"

Jake eyed me curiously. "Why do you ask?"

"I'm not going to beat around the bush. Ronnie is in serious danger. Someone's trying to kill her. We think it has something to do with her engine, and we think someone directly related to the oil industry is behind it. You're in a position to bring her engine to fruition. People in high places know that." I looked at Craig. "Some people believe love can be more persuasive than the promise of money, or even the threat of death."

Jake let out a half-hearted laugh. "You've been watching too many conspiracy theory movies. These people you're talking about are not vampires hiding in the shadows, waiting to suck the blood out of poor unsuspecting souls. They're businessmen and women. They have families and homes, just like everyone else. They're not a bunch of bloodthirsty criminals, like you're making them out to be."

"Right. They're just like you and me. They live by the golden rule," Ronnie said, her voice heavy with sarcasm.

"Do unto others?" I asked.

"No. The one with all the gold, rules," Ronnie replied, looking directly at Jake.

Craig began gathering the empty dinner plates and stacking them. "We're not saying every person in the oil business is behind the attempts on Ronnie's life. But someone seems to be acting on behalf of the industry. It's just too coincidental that so many inventors have been killed after filing patents that could be damaging to their business," Craig said.

"I think it's some misguided lunatic. Probably saw her at one of Lance's races and decided to stalk her. You know, some redneck who can't stand the thought of a woman with her hands on an engine," Jake speculated.

"That doesn't explain all the others," Ronnie argued.

Before Jake could continue, the doorbell rang. I was relieved for the interruption. All the arguing had begun to wear on my nerves. I got up from the table and went to answer the door.

Two uniformed officers stood in the glow of the porch light on the front step. I gaped for a moment, waiting for them to announce their business.

"We're here for Veronica Oakhurst," the taller one said.

"Ronnie? What for?" I asked.

"Ma'am, we have a warrant. Please step aside," the officer continued, pushing his way past me into the foyer. I noted the names engraved on brass plates pinned to their uniforms. The tall one's name was Pianalto and the other was Hollers.

"Wait a minute," I demanded. "Let me see this warrant."

Officer Hollers handed me an official-looking paper as he followed Pianalto into the house. I skimmed over it as quickly as I could.

"Who is it?" Craig called from the dining room.

I didn't answer. I was busy trying to make sense of the warrant.

Craig strolled out of the dining room to find out for himself who'd come calling. His face showed surprise at the sight of the two officers. "What is it?" Craig asked.

"Where is Veronica Oakhurst? We have a warrant for her arrest," Pianalto said.

"What?" Craig blurted.

The officers, impatient with our ignorance, made their way into the dining room. Craig and I followed.

"Veronica Oakhurst?" Hollers asked, looking directly at Ronnie seated at the table.

"Yes?" she meekly replied, confused.

"Please stand up," Hollers demanded. "You're under arrest for the production of methamphetamine at your residence in Ramona."

Jake gaped at the scene. "Methamphetamine? That's ridiculous," he stated, emphatically.

I handed Craig the warrant and headed for the phone in the kitchen. I dialed Sam's number and counted the rings. He picked up on the third one.

"Sam. It's Devonie. What's the big idea?" I blurted into the phone.

"Hello to you, too," he replied. "How nice to hear your friendly voice."

"Never mind the nice-nice act. What the heck do you think you're doing, arresting Ronnie?" I demanded.

"What?"

I glanced around the corner to see what was going on in the dining room. Ronnie was being searched for weapons.

"You know what I mean. There are two policemen in my house at this very moment, frisking Ronnie and getting ready to haul her away," I hissed.

"Who? I didn't order it," he insisted.

"Pianalto and Hollers," I said.

"Pian . . . who? I never heard of them. What precinct?"

"You don't know them?"

"No. You check their IDs?"

I stepped around the corner into the dining room. Pian-alto had Ronnie by the arm and was leading her toward the front door. Hollers removed a pair of handcuffs from his back pocket and was ready to place them on Ronnie's wrists. "Stop," I said. "Check their IDs," I told Craig.

Hollers gave his partner an irritated look. The muscles in his neck tensed. I noticed a lightning bolt-shaped scar under his right ear—probably a work-related injury. I could tell Pianalto didn't want to turn loose his prisoner to re-move the identification from his pocket, but he complied. He motioned for Hollers to show his. Hollers pulled a leather wallet from his pocket and flipped it open for Craig to inspect. Jake peered over his shoulder to get a look at the badges.

"What precinct?" I asked.

Craig studied the ID, then looked up at me. "Ninety-eighth?" he said, his voice unsure.

"Ninety-eighth precinct," I repeated into the phone.

Pianalto pushed Ronnie toward the door, in a hurry to get her outside.

"Ninety-eighth? Stop them. It's bogus," Sam blurted into my ear.

I ran toward the front door. "Stop! They're not for real! Don't let them take her!" I yelled as Pianalto and Hollers began dragging Ronnie at a full run toward their car. Craig and Jake sprinted after them.

I watched in horror as Hollers let go of Ronnie's arm and pulled out the gun holstered under his arm. He aimed it directly at Craig's head.

"No!" I screamed.

Craig stood, motionless. Jake didn't make a move. Everything seemed to happen in slow motion from that moment on.

Ronnie, still in Pianalto's grip, let out a high-pitched scream and kicked her foot up well above her waist, hitting Hollers in the wrist and knocking the gun from his hand. Before he could recover, she kicked him again, square in the middle of his chest, the blow throwing him backwards a good ten feet before he landed hard on the ground. She'd managed to free one hand and reached back toward Pianalto's right ear. The next thing I knew, Pianalto was flying over her shoulder and landed flat on his back. She placed her foot across his throat and grabbed for the gun in his holster. The gun was strapped into the holster so she couldn't get it out. She jerked on it, but her awkward position wouldn't let it come free. By this time, Hollers was up and heading for his gun. Jake saw this and dove for the gun, reaching it seconds before Hollers could get his hands on it. Jake aimed the gun at Hollers. Hollers put his hands up in a gesture of surrender, then backed toward the car. He opened the driver-side door and slid in. Pianalto knew his partner was abandoning him when he heard the engine start. He shoved Ronnie off balance so her foot came free of his throat. He jumped to his feet and lunged for the back door of the car as it sped away. He managed to get the door open and let it drag him a few feet before he was able to jump into the back seat and escape with his partner.

Jake rushed to Ronnie's side and put his arms around her. "Are you okay?"

She buried her face in his chest and started sobbing.

I leaped over a row of young azaleas and put a hand on Craig's arm. "How about you? Are you alright?"

Craig just gawked and pointed at Ronnie. Finally, he found his voice. "She's my hero. Did you see that? She took those guys out like they were a couple of Raggedy Andy dolls," he said in marvel.

I smiled. "I know. I think she may have saved your life."

"I think you're right."

Jake walked Ronnie back into the house. Craig and I followed.

Ronnie stopped and took hold of Jake's arm, turning him to face her. "Are you still sure it's some misguided lunatic?"

Jake's face was troubled.

"The question is, how did they find you here?" I asked.

Jake's shoulders slumped. He slowly walked toward a chair in the living room and collapsed into it. We followed him, curious about his sudden depression.

"What is it, Jake?" Ronnie asked.

"I'm afraid they found you because they followed me here," he said.

"Followed you?" Craig asked.

Jake nodded. "It didn't hit me until Devonie told us they were imposters. The one called Hollers looked familiar to me, but I figured he was just someone who looked like someone. You know? But it's not that. I've seen him before. I can't remember where, but I know it's him."

Ronnie kneeled on the floor next to Jake. He put a hand on her shoulder.

"I'm so sorry, Ronnie. I led them right to you. It's all my fault."

Chapter Nine

Sam took a description of the two men who posed as police officers, and also the car they used.

Jake sat close to Ronnie on the sofa and held her hand while we all told Sam our own versions of what took place with the imposters.

"Any word about her brother?" Sam asked.

"Not yet. Rick and Gary said they'd call us once they got there, but we haven't heard anything yet," I told him.

Sam scratched his head. "Hmm. Should've been there by now. Maybe they had phone trouble."

"Maybe," I replied, unconvinced.

"She's probably not safe here, you know," Sam reminded me.

"I know."

He closed his notebook and stuffed it into his pocket. "Want me to see if we can put her up somewhere? A motel maybe?"

I stared out the window toward the dock. I shook my head. "No. I think we've got things covered."

Sam followed my line of sight and gazed at the *Plan C*, tied to the private dock we shared with my Uncle Doug, who lived next door. He nodded with understanding. "You be careful. These guys are serious."

Craig stood up to walk Sam to the door. "Don't worry. I won't let anything happen to them."

Sam gave him a doubtful glance and then let himself out.

Craig closed the door and turned to face us. "Okay people. Let's get busy," he said, rubbing his hands together like a magician preparing to pull a rabbit out of a hat.

My first assigned task was to secure a suitable sitter for the puppy. I loaded his dog crate and a forty-pound bag of Puppy Chow in a wagon. Then, I heaved the puppy over my shoulder, grabbed the handle of the wagon, and headed for Uncle Doug's house. I rang the bell and put on my biggest smile.

"Hi, Uncle Doug," I said, shifting the puppy to my other shoulder.

"Well, hello there. Who's this?" he asked, reaching out to pat the puppy's head.

"This is . . . puppy. He hasn't got a name yet. Craig gave him to me for our six-month anniversary."

Uncle Doug gave him one more pat, then peered around me at the wagonload of Puppy Chow I'd tried, unsuccessfully, to hide behind a shrub. "Are you taking him on a trip?" he asked, eyeing me suspiciously.

"No," I said, lifting the heavy puppy a little higher on my shoulder.

"Can I ask why you—"

"I need a favor, Uncle Doug. It's sort of an emergency."

* * *

Uncle Doug reluctantly agreed to puppy-sit for me only after Aunt Arlene came to my rescue and insisted. She had a soft spot for animals and there was no way she would allow that sweet little creature to be locked up in a boarding kennel.

Craig, Jake, and Ronnie loaded the *Plan C* with food and supplies while I took care of puppy business. The 60-foot sailing yacht had four double cabins, each with their own private heads. She also had a fully-equipped galley, and every piece of navigation equipment imaginable. Craig and I had become a pretty good team at sailing her.

I double-checked the supplies and made sure we had plenty of fuel. I also checked the dinghy's fuel level. Our dinghy for this trip would be Craig's 19-foot Sea Ray. I checked that the towline was secure. Everything seemed in good working order—the generator, the navigation equipment, and the radios.

We made one last trip from the house to the boat. Craig stopped to set the alarm and lock the door behind us. He'd changed into a pair of green shorts, a Hawaiian shirt, and a straw hat he bought when we were in the Caribbean last year. The colorful hat had a woven basket on each side, designed to hold two drinks. The face of a rat decorated the front of the hat, complete with a cone-shaped nose jutting out over the brim. A fake rat tail hung off the back. It's so hideous; I laugh every time I look at it. He turned around and caught me standing there, admiring his Sunday-sailor outfit. He grinned and winked at me. "Bet you wish you could achieve this same suave, sophisticated look," he boasted.

I smiled and patted him on the behind as he walked past me. "Honey, there's no way I could ever look as good as you do in that hat."

We set sail for San Diego and dropped anchor a mile off shore, not far from the marina where I used to live on the *Plan C* before Craig and I were married.

Craig pulled chef duty the first night, which meant he cooked dinner with the help of Jake. Ronnie and I cleaned up afterwards.

The next morning, while Craig got ready for work, I instructed Ronnie and Jake on the use of the radio equipment, in case they needed help. Craig left his cell phone with them, and I kept mine with me. I gave them all the necessary phone numbers to call in case of any emergency.

I grabbed my laptop computer and followed Craig onto the Sea Ray. "We'll be back this afternoon," I called to Ronnie and Jake as Craig started the motor and we sped away. Ronnie stood on the deck of the *Plan C* and waved goodbye, like a child watching her balloon fly away, never to return.

Mr. Cartwright, my neighbor when I lived at the marina, let us tie the Sea Ray up in his slip. He even offered to drive Craig to the hospital, but Craig had made arrangements to have one of the other doctors pick him up.

I took him up on his offer for a ride, though. I had planned to call a taxi, but Mr. Cartwright insisted. He dropped me off at the Lace Marina, where Uncle Doug owned a yacht brokerage.

Uncle Doug glanced at me over his reading glasses as I walked into his office.

"Good morning," I said.

"If you say so," he replied.

I gave him a closer inspection. He had heavy bags under both eyes, which were a little bloodshot. "What's wrong? You look like you just pulled an all-nighter."

"What's wrong? Let me tell you what's wrong. Arlene woke me up every hour on the hour last night to take *your* puppy outside. He had one accident in the house, and let me tell you, I've seen smaller 'mistakes' made by elephants."

I cringed as he described his evening to me. I felt terrible. "I'm sorry, Uncle Doug. Why didn't you put him in his crate at bedtime like I told you?" I asked.

"Arlene wouldn't let me. I'm lucky she didn't have him in bed with us."

"Well, tonight put him in his crate. He's used to that. He won't give you any problem."

"No, but Arlene will."

"Tell her he likes his crate. It's like his crib. He has toys in there. And I'll pay to have your carpets cleaned. I'm really sorry."

"Don't worry about it. How'd you do last night? Any trouble?"

"No. Smooth sailing." I set my laptop case on the corner of his desk.

"What's that?" he asked.

"My laptop. Can I borrow your DSL line?"

"You need to get on the Internet?" he asked.

"Yeah."

"Why don't you use my PC? It's all set up," he offered.

"I have some special software loaded on mine."

He frowned. "Special software?"

I nodded, hoping he wouldn't ask any more questions. My conscience wouldn't let me keep silent. "I need to get some information from . . . well, you probably don't want to know. I'm not going to hurt anyone. I just want to take a look at some records," I explained.

"You're going to be hacking on my DSL line?"

"Only if you say yes. If you prefer, I can go back home and use our old-fashioned phone line. It'll only take me about a week to download what I need."

He shook his head. "No. No. Go ahead. If someone asks, I'll just claim ignorance."

"Thanks, Uncle Doug. You're a lifesaver."

I'd called Spencer, my computer-hacker friend, last night to see if he had any advice on how I could get the information I was after. I was convinced Spencer could hack into any computer on earth, given enough time. He e-mailed me a 'Trojan horse' program he'd written. He was so proud; you'd think he'd just written an Oscar-winning screenplay. I scrolled through the code and shook my head. Spencer was a genius, but he was a sloppy programmer. He strung lines of code out for miles and didn't line anything up for easy reading. Once, I made a passing comment about his sloppiness, and you'd have thought I called his baby ugly.

Uncle Doug watched with guarded curiosity as I logged onto the Internet and began navigating to the web sites of most of the major oil companies. I looked for links to contact names, or better yet, e-mail addresses of employees within the companies.

"What are you doing now?" he asked.

"I'm compiling a list of e-mail addresses. As many as I can."

"Why?"

I continued clicking on the links, writing down names. "I'm going to send them a message."

"A message?" he asked, confused.

"Yes. And attached to the message will be a special program. A 'Trojan horse.' I'll disguise it as something else, so they won't be afraid of it."

"Disguise it?" he continued, taking a seat next to me.

"Yes. I'll make it look like a harmless text file. Maybe some warning not to lick envelopes, or sit in movie theater seats, or talk to strangers in shopping mall parking lots. Doesn't matter. I just need them to open it."

"What happens once they open it?" he asked.

"The 'Trojan horse' will install itself on their computer. It'll give me backdoor access to their system. I'll hunt around for the files I need, download what I want, then remove the 'Trojan' so they'll never even know they've been hacked."

"Won't a virus checker stop it?" Uncle Doug asked, looking more concerned than ever.

"Not this one. It's a scrap file. Most virus checkers don't scan for these," I explained.

I finished compiling my list of e-mail addresses and began my fishing expedition—casting out the message and hoping a good percentage of the recipients would take the bait by double-clicking on the file attachment. I used the name of the United States Surgeon General as the sender, and the subject line read *Urgent warning about health risks and exposure to petroleum products.*

Employees from four of the major companies were curious enough to at least open the file attachment I sent. I was able to gain access to General Oil, Chevport, Extan, and Shoal. Once in their system, I simply had to locate the accounts payable and payroll tables. Since all the companies I'd targeted used one of three major software packages available for large process manufacturing plants, locating the tables was not difficult. The table names were intuitive, to make system maintenance manageable. I copied the vendor master tables, accounts payable history tables, employee tables and payroll history tables to my laptop.

The whole process took most of the day. I checked my watch as I packed up my laptop. "I better hurry. Craig will be waiting for me at the marina."

"I'll give you a lift. I'm ready to close up shop here. Just let me lock up," Uncle Doug said.

This time, it was Ronnie and Jake's turn to fix dinner. They'd spent the morning fishing, so their catch became our meal. Craig stood by in the kitchen to help direct them to the utensils they'd need.

I got busy transferring the data I'd downloaded from the oil companies' servers into my own database. I converted the data from the various tables into a common format so I could perform comparisons on each of the columns.

After dinner, Craig took Ronnie and Jake out on the deck to look at the stars. I went back to work on my project. I started by comparing the employee tables from all the companies. I wanted to know if any of them shared a common employee—someone on the payroll to do their dirty work. I compared names, addresses, birth dates, and Social Security numbers. I found a few employees who'd worked for several of the oil companies over the years, but their employment dates didn't overlap. It looked like they left one company to work for another. *Not unusual*, I thought.

Ronnie, Jake, and Craig came in from outside when their jackets were no longer able to fend off the chill.

"Any luck?" Ronnie asked as she plopped down in a chair next to me and gazed at the computer screen.

"Not yet," I answered. "But I still have to check the vendor and accounts payable tables."

"What are you looking for?" Jake asked.

"A common denominator. Something they all share," I explained.

"How do you do that?" Ronnie asked.

I felt somehow proud that I actually knew something that Ronnie didn't. She was a genius in my eyes, and up until now, I felt rather dim in her presence.

"Here. I'll show you." I executed a query to compare vendor names from all the companies. Whenever it found the same name in more than one table, it would return a row to the screen.

Craig and Jake moved around to get a better look.

Craig read the names as they displayed on the screen. "AT and T, Airborne, Fed Ex, Federal Express, United Airlines, United Parcel Service, UPS. Why are some listed more than once?"

"Because these companies spell the names out, and those companies use acronyms or abbreviations. Any variations will produce separate results," I explained.

Ronnie studied the list. "Those weren't UPS delivery men the other night at your house."

"I know," I said. "You would expect to see these vendors being used for most American companies. There's nothing surprising here."

"So that's it? You're done?" Jake asked.

"Not hardly. We still have to compare contact names, phone numbers, vendor addresses, 'remit to' addresses, 'deliver from' addresses, and tax ID numbers," I said.

"How long will that take?" Ronnie asked.

"Not long, providing I enter my query correctly."

There were no surprises when I queried the contact names. I also specifically looked for Charlie Johnston, Jack Pearle, Pianalto, and Hollers. No matches were found.

I didn't get any hits comparing the vendor addresses, the "deliver from" addresses or the tax IDs. I saved the "remit to" addresses for last, because that's where I felt we had the best chance of finding something. That's where the money goes. I started first by including two addresses, city, state, and zip code in my comparison. There were no results returned. Then, I dropped one of the addresses. Still no results. When I excluded both addresses, as I suspected, hundreds of rows were returned. Every vendor in every major city in the country came up in the list. I sorted the results by city and began the tedious task of looking for a common thread.

Atlanta—nothing. Austin—nothing. Baltimore—nothing. Boston—nothing. Chicago—nothing. Dallas—nothing. Denver—nothing. Then, we all read the next city name aloud. "Graeagle?"

"Where's Graeagle?" Jake asked.

"California. Up north," I said. "It's a little retirement community in the Sierras. Golf courses, country clubs, lots of rich old geezers."

"And rich young yuppies," Craig added.

"I've never heard of it," Ronnie said.

"I only know about it because my Uncle Doug owns a house up there. He rents it out most of the year. He lets me use it whenever I feel like I want to escape the congestion of the big city. It's a beautiful place."

Craig studied the list closer. "Seems a little strange that all these big oil companies would have business with different entities in such a secluded little place."

"I agree," I said. I reprocessed the query, limiting the results to include only Graeagle, and then printed the list. All the company addresses were post office boxes. No physical addresses were recorded.

"All four oil companies had relationships with four different businesses in Graeagle. Let's see what kind of money we're talking about," I said as I formulated another query to search the accounts payable history table for total dollar amounts paid to each of the four businesses in the tiny town. I pressed the GO button and waited for the results.

"Holy cow," I said as the amounts scrolled up the screen. "Look at this. In the last fiscal year, each of these outfits received over five million dollars from their respective oil company. What in the world do they do for that kind of money?"

Craig read down the list. "CII? IMI? Elite Incorporated? Power Makers Corporation? I can't tell from the company names what sort of businesses they are."

I typed in another query. "I think I can take care of that. We'll look at individual checks. Hopefully, they put some sort of notations on the ledger distribution. The accountants hate it when things aren't documented."

I submitted the query and hundreds of rows scrolled up the screen. I found the column I'd named COMMENTS and began reading down the list. "Television shoots? Magazine interviews? Ads? Commercials? These are all public relations companies, I think."

Jake pounded his fist down on the arm of the chair. "That's it! That's where I've seen Hollers before," he exclaimed. "They'd been filming."

"Who was filming?" Ronnie asked.

"Extan Oil. After that big oil spill fiasco. They had to do something to improve their image. Remember?" Jake continued, excited.

"I remember. Who could forget? All those poor animals killed because of the oil slick," Craig said.

"I had a meeting with the Extan CEO. Gosh, that was about seven years ago," Jake said.

"What sort of meeting?" I asked.

"Who can remember? They're always the same. They buy me an expensive lunch, give me a bunch of expensive gifts, thank me for keeping their interests at the forefront of my decision-making. You know, the same old bull."

Craig scratched his head. "Where does Hollers come into the picture?"

"He delayed my meeting. I cooled my heels in some assistant's office while he had an impromptu session with the CEO. Hollers never saw me, but I saw him. He had to deliver a video his company had just completed. They wanted to get it on the air right away, but the CEO had to approve it first. After Hollers left, I got to see the video for myself."

"It was Hollers?" I asked.

"I'm sure of it. That lightning bolt scar on the side of his neck stuck in my mind," Jake said.

"What was on the video?" Ronnie asked.

Jake shook his head and gave a half-hearted chuckle. "You know that commercial that shows a dumping ground at the bottom of the ocean where Extan had discarded a bunch of used pipe and equipment they could no longer use?"

I nodded. "The one where an ecosystem had developed and a whole little community of fish and other sea life had set up house in the junk?"

"That's the one," Jake said, pointing at me. "As if the ecosystem developed *because* of the garbage they dumped rather than *in spite* of it."

I nodded. "I remember that commercial. I thought it was

kind of weird that they'd admit to dumping the stuff in the first place."

"I think they got caught and someone was going to go public with it. They put every resource they had into damage control. They scrambled to get that commercial on the air before the whistle-blowers could," Jake said.

I scrolled across the screen to the company name listed for Extan's check. "CII. So Hollers works for this company?"

"He did then. As I recall, CII is an acronym for Corporate Images, Incorporated," Jake said.

I shut down the laptop and started packing it back in its case. "I wonder how Mr. Hollers's job description reads. 'Job skill requirements: deliveries, impersonations, bombs, arson, kidnapping—murder'?"

Chapter Ten

T he next morning, Craig and I climbed onto the Sea Ray and headed in for another day on the mainland. We pulled up to Mr. Cartwright's slip and cut the engine. I spotted Craig's colleague waiting for him in the marina parking lot.

"What's on your agenda today?" Craig asked, as he tied the line to a ring on the dock.

"I thought I'd go by the house and check the mail and our phone messages. I want to visit the puppy. Give Aunt Arlene a break. He hasn't been a perfect angel."

Craig frowned. "He's just a puppy. He'll grow up to be a good dog. We really have to come up with a name for him."

"I know. I'm working on it."

"I want you to be careful if you're going by the house. No telling who might be watching the place," Craig warned.

"I'll be fine," I assured him.

"I mean it, Dev. Why don't you just wait? We can check the answering machine remotely. The mail can wait a couple days."

"When did you become such a worrywart?" I asked as I climbed over the edge of the boat onto the wet dock. My foot slipped and I started to fall.

"Whoa there," Craig said, as he grabbed me to save me from plunging into the water. "I became a worrywart the day I met you. I discovered your obvious knack for finding trouble and decided someone had to keep an eye on you."

His arms were still wrapped around me, even though I'd regained my balance and was no longer in danger of falling. I smiled at him. "Don't worry about me too much. I wouldn't want your hair to turn prematurely gray. People might think you're a cradle robber."

I gave him a kiss and sent him on his way.

My friend Jason agreed to give me a ride to our house before he opened up his shop. I waited in the marina office for 20 minutes before his pickup rattled into the parking lot. I pointed to my watch as his truck rolled to a stop next to the sidewalk.

"You're late," I complained.

"Nag, nag, nag. You don't know how glad I am that Craig's the one who got stuck with you."

"Good morning to you too," I replied.

He picked up a brown bag, soaked with spots of grease, and held it out to me. "I brought breakfast."

I crinkled my nose at the oily sack. "I ate. Thanks."

"You sure? It's really good," he coaxed.

"What is it?" I asked.

" 'What is it?' Beggars can't be choosers. I had to stop

at three places to get the right food groups. I hoped you'd be a little appreciative."

"I'm not a beggar. I told you I already ate. I'm just curious what you're subjecting your poor arteries to this fine morning."

"It's spicy deep-fried potato wedges, bacon-wrapped cocktail weenies and apple turnovers. That's fruit, you know."

I grimaced. "Fruit? Right. And grease and sugar and preservatives and nitrates and artificial colors and artificial flavors and—"

"Hey. You know what I always say. 'Eat well. Stay fit. Die anyway.' "

I shook my head. Time to change the subject. I'd grown tired of harping at Jason about his eating habits. It was his body, I'd decided. I wasn't his keeper. "How's business?" I asked.

"Booming. I might have to hire a third repairman. People are opting to fix their washers and dryers these days, instead of throwing them out to buy new ones. Good for me, but I'm working too many hours."

I spent the next 20 minutes telling Jason about Ronnie's predicament. When I described her inventions to him, he nearly called me a liar.

"Impossible. Take it from me. I know motors. What you're describing is impossible. It defies all the laws of physics," he proclaimed.

"I've seen it. I'm telling you, she's done it," I argued.

"She's tricked you. Believe me. It can't be done."

I crossed my arms over my chest. "Right. And how many years was the earth flat? And remember when the universe revolved around the earth? And it was impossible for man to fly? That was a gift only given to birds. Heaven forbid anyone ever set foot on the moon."

"That's different," he defended.

"How so?" I demanded.

Jason was silent.

"What's the matter? Cat got your tongue?"

"I'm thinking. I'm thinking," he insisted.

"No, you're not. That's the problem."

The argument continued until we pulled to a stop in front of Uncle Doug's house. As soon as Jason set his parking brake, the dispute ended. He gave me the same concerned look he always does when he learns of my latest escapade.

"You got a ride back to the marina?" Jason asked.

"I'll get one. Thanks," I said, letting myself out of his truck.

I can't describe the feeling I had when Aunt Arlene opened the door for me and let me into her house. The puppy stopped playing with his chew-toy for a moment to see who the new person in the house was. When he saw me, he dropped everything and bounded across the living room at breakneck speed to greet me. My heart leaped in my chest. He actually recognized me and seemed to be elated. Then, he nearly knocked me down when he jumped on me.

I told Aunt Arlene I'd take him for a walk and keep him with me until I had to return to the marina. She didn't say so, but I think she was relieved for the break. She had some shopping to do, and was happy she didn't have to lock him in his crate while she was out.

I did my best to wear the puppy out on our walk. I took him down to the water to see if he'd take any interest in swimming. I tossed a stick into the water a few feet, but he wouldn't go in after it. I didn't push it.

I tossed the stack of mail and my house keys onto the kitchen table. After giving the puppy a couple of doggie cookies, I strolled into the den. It felt so good to have room to move around. I never noticed feeling overly confined when I lived on my boat, but now that I lived in a house, I didn't think I could go back to living in that small space again. I checked the answering machine. We had two messages. I pressed the playback button and listened.

The first message was from Bo Rawlings, the patent holder I tried to contact days before. His attorney must have gotten my message to him. He left a number where he could be reached. I replayed the message and wrote the number down. He'd called last night, around 8:00.

The next message was from Rick Caper. "Hi. This is Rick from Caper and Lawless. Anyone there? I think we got something here, but I need to talk to you. I'll try one of the other numbers you gave us. Bye." He'd called this morning, not long before I'd arrived home. I checked my watch. If I'd spent less time trying to convince the puppy that the water was perfectly safe, I probably wouldn't have missed the call.

I dialed Bo Rawlings' number and waited for an answer.

"Hello? Mr. Rawlings?" I asked.

"Yes," he answered.

"Hi. My name is Devonie Lace . . . Matthews . . . Lace-Matthews. Your attorney gave you a message to call me."

"Right. I called last night. What can I do for you?" he asked.

I sat down at the desk and removed a pad of paper and

a pen from the drawer. "I'm interested in the patent you filed back in nineteen eighty-nine. For the engine?"

"Oh, that. I'm sorry. I sold that patent a long time ago. You're about ten years too late," he said.

I noted down the "ten year" reference. "I wasn't really interested in buying the patent. I'm more interested in who bought it from you."

There was a brief silence. "Can I ask why you want to know?" he said.

I bit my lip and searched my imagination to find the perfect excuse for wanting to know. Would it hurt to tell him the truth? That I suspect the rich and powerful oil companies are killing inventors who threaten their business? "I have a friend with a patent for an engine. She's a little strapped for money and is interested in selling it. I found out you sold yours, and wondered if you had any suggestions who she might contact."

"Really? What sort of engine?" he asked, his interest piqued.

"I believe she calls it a 'heat exchange' engine. Entropy?" I said.

He laughed. "Heat exchange? She won't find anyone interested in buying that. You couldn't power a boat's trolling motor with the horsepower you'd get out of it."

I tapped the end of the pen on the tablet of paper, wondering how I should proceed. "Hmm. That's not what she told me. Are you sure about this?"

He chuckled again. "Sure as I am that the sun rises in the east. Tell you what. Movell Oil bought my patent. I doubt they'd be interested in your friend's idea, but there are others who might. A few people had contacted me back before I sold the patent. One guy was pretty persistent. Really interested in any new technology. I have his number here, somewhere," he said. I could hear him fumbling with papers. "Here it is. Jack Pearle. You got a pen?"

My ears perked up. "Jack Pearle, you said?"

"That's right. You know him?"

"No. But you have his number?" I asked.

"Yeah. Address too. It's ten years old. Don't know if he's still in business, but you can give it a try."

I wrote down the number and address. He chatted for a while longer, filling me in on the details of the sale of his own patent. Movell Oil paid him a small fortune for his patent—enough to set up a nice little cattle ranch on one of the Hawaiian Islands. He and his family were living a fantasy island dream—perpetual green pastures, beautiful horses, fat cows, and no worries.

I asked him if the oil company had ever done anything with his engine idea. "Now, why would they?" he asked, laughing, as if it were a stupid question.

"Right. Well, thanks again," I said.

There was no answer at the number Rawlings gave me for Jack Pearle. At least there was no recording that it had been disconnected. I thought I'd give it another try in 30 minutes.

I took the puppy out back to play. By the time we finished five rounds of tug-of-war and another eight games of fetch, he was ready for a nap.

When I tried Jack Pearle's number again, there still was no answer. I powered up my PC and entered the address Bo Rawlings gave me into a mapping program. I printed out the directions, shut everything down, collected the puppy, and headed for the door. I set the alarm.

I started for Uncle Doug's house, when I remembered

that Aunt Arlene had left to go shopping. She hadn't returned yet.

"Wanna go for a ride?" I said to the puppy, trying to raise some excitement. He hadn't learned what that sentence meant yet. I unlocked my Explorer and loaded him into the back seat. He plopped down and promptly closed his eyes.

The address for Jack Pearle's business was in a small industrial park in Los Angeles. I made a slow drive-by past the place to check it out. It looked legit, though there were no signs indicating that Pearle Manufacturing had anything to do with the place. In fact, there were no signs at all, just the unit number stenciled on the door.

I parked in an open spot in front of another unit across from Pearle's. "You stay here. I'll be right back," I said over my shoulder to the puppy, who was still resting comfortably in the back seat. He lifted his head and slapped his tail twice on the cushion, then laid it back down and closed his eyes.

I tried the door, but it was locked. I knocked, but couldn't raise anyone. I peered through the window next to the door to see inside. It was dark, but I could make out plenty of machinery. It looked like a genuine machine shop. I didn't see any sign of life inside. I checked my watch. All the other businesses in the complex were busy attending to their enterprises. Where was Jack Pearle? I thought I'd try asking one of his neighbors, when a hand on my shoulder startled me almost out of my skin.

"Something I can do for you?" the gruff voice said as I spun around.

"Jeez. You scared me," I gasped, clutching my hand to my chest.

"Snooping women scare me. Guess we're even," he replied.

I took a step back. "I wasn't snooping. I'm looking for Jack Pearle. You know him?" I asked.

"Who wants to know?"

"My name's Devonie. You know him?" I repeated.

"I'm Jack. What is it you want?"

Jack Pearle stood about six feet tall. His thick white hair was combed back from his face and cut short. His hair looked even whiter against his deeply tanned face. He looked as though he spent most of his time outdoors. His bushy eyebrows shaded his pale blue eyes from the bright morning sun. His features were striking. I estimated him to be somewhere in his 60's. Even at his age, he was a handsome man, and I was sure that in his younger days, he attracted a fair number of women.

"I understand you buy engine patents?" I asked.

He studied me. "Maybe. You have one to sell?"

I shook my head. "You contacted Ronnie Oakhurst a while back. Remember?"

He scratched his chin. "Yeah. Liked the look of her idea. Wouldn't sell, though." He pulled a set of keys from his pocket. "Come on inside. I'm late opening up."

I glanced around at the other businesses buzzing away. I felt safe out in the open with people wandering around. Witnesses. "I'd rather stay outside, if you don't mind."

He gave me a curious look. I pointed toward my Ford. "I've left my dog in the car. I want to keep an eye on him," I said.

He nodded, seeming to understand. "Do you know Ronnie Oakhurst?" he asked.

"Yes. But I'll get to the point. Hers isn't the only patent you've tried to buy. How many patents do you own?"

Jack Pearle frowned. "I don't own any. Can't get anyone to partner with me, and I ain't got the capital to compete with the big guns."

Big guns. Interesting choice of words. "You've been trying for a long time. None of the patent holders has agreed to partner with you?"

"Oh, a lot of them get excited and say they'll do it. But then they get an offer they can't refuse, and it's 'goodbye Jack.' "

I nodded. "I tried to find your phone number in the yellow pages, but you're not listed. And there's no sign," I said.

"I'm semi-retired. Pearle Manufacturing is on its way out. Mostly just a hobby now. I do a little work for the neighbors. Pays the rent and the electricity bills, but that's about it."

We spent the next 30 minutes talking about the potential for an engine that could produce as much horsepower as an internal combustion engine without the fossil fuel restrictions. The cost savings. The benefits to the environment. The independence awarded to the public. I got the impression that Jack Pearle would like to be a part of that revolution. That was the reason he'd spent so many years trying to partner with the right person—someone like Ronnie.

"You know what? I hope the price of gasoline goes to five bucks a gallon," Jack said, apparently trying to shock me.

"Five bucks? Why on earth would you want that?" I replied.

" 'Cause I want to know just how much the people of this country will take. There has to be some point when they get fed up and do something. Remember the Boston

Tea Party? Where's that spirit now? We've turned into a bunch of pathetic pushovers."

Jack's eyes flashed and his passion rose like an evangelist preaching to the sinners of the world to change their ways or face the inevitable. "I bet five bucks won't even do it. They'll all just whine louder as they fill their tanks and take out loans to pay their electric bills."

I listened to his sermon without saying a word, but I wanted to raise my hands and holler "Amen!" on several occasions.

"You know," he continued, "everyone says the government ought to step in and fix it. Well that's just a bunch of hogwash. What is it with this country? We pay our taxes then we wash our hands of it, as if the politicians in Washington have all the answers. We pay people to do the stuff we don't want to deal with, then we're stuck with the results. Heck, my son-in-law doesn't even know his car *has* sparkplugs, let alone how to change them. You believe that? We pay people to raise our kids, fix our food, clean our houses, then we moan and groan because our kids turn out to be criminals, our diets make us fat, and our housekeepers rob us blind. But what do we do about it? We hire consultants to analyze. We spend more money to have someone else solve the problem. Only problem is, the problem never gets solved. It just changes to a new problem."

He calmed down and his voice relaxed. "What this country needs is an attitude adjustment. That's what I say. Fed up? Don't get mad. Get independent."

I nodded in agreement, but the magnitude of the obstacle keeping the people from independence seemed overwhelming. My thought was that Jack was right. Five dollars, six dollars, even ten dollars a gallon might not be enough to spur the people to overcome the powers that be.

I turned my eyes toward my Ford at the sound of a bark. A pair of brown eyes and a big black nose pressed against the window tried hard to get my attention. I motioned toward the Ford. "There's my signal to head home. Thanks for your time, Mr. Pearle," I said, heading off toward the Explorer.

"Wait a minute," he called after me. "What's this all about?"

I opened my door. "Nothing yet. Can I call you if I have more questions?" I called back to him.

He nodded, confused, and then watched me drive away.

I spent the rest of the day hanging around the house, keeping the puppy company. I spent an hour trying different names on him. Zeus. Zeke. Moose. Rex, as in Tyrannosaurus. Nothing seemed to stick. I checked the clock. It was almost time to meet Craig.

I carried the puppy back to Aunt Arlene's and asked if she'd mind giving me a ride to the marina.

Craig was already there, waiting for me at Mr. Cartwright's slip. I untied the lines and jumped aboard as he started the engine. We puttered along slowly through the rows of boats. I told him about my day, and my conversation with Jack Pearle.

"You went to see him alone?" he asked.

"Yes. It was fine, honey. He's harmless."

"But you didn't know that. I wish you'd wait for me before you go confronting these guys."

I slid closer to him and inspected his head. "Uh-oh. There's another gray hair."

He grinned at me. We were out of the marina's slow speed zone. He pushed the throttle forward, and I nearly lost my balance. I was forced to grab hold of his waist to keep from falling.

Craig eased back on the throttle. I retrieved a pair of binoculars. We both scanned the horizon. The smiles left our faces. "It's not in sight," I said, handing him the field glasses. The *Plan C* was gone.

Chapter Eleven

The Sea Ray skimmed the surface of the water as we sped back to the marina. A million thoughts raced through my mind. Had someone found Ronnie hiding on the *Plan C* and taken her? Had they finished the job they tried to do earlier, the one that landed Ronnie in the hospital? Could Ronnie and Jake and the *Plan C* be sitting on the bottom of the ocean? I didn't want to imagine the worst, but I couldn't keep those thoughts from flashing through my mind.

Craig eased back on the throttle as we approached the marina. We made our way slowly through the rows of boats. We decided to return to the marina to ask around if anyone had seen the *Plan C* during the day. We'd barely passed the first row of larger vessels when I spotted her.

"Look! There she is," I said, pointing toward the end of the third row of boats. The *Plan C* was nestled between two larger boats. I wouldn't have even noticed her, except an angry sailor was trying to dock his boat, and apparently, the *Plan C* was in his slip.

"I'll move her," I called to the irate sailor. "My friends mistook this slip for mine. Sorry."

He forced a smile and waited while I fired up the engine and slowly moved the large sailboat out of his space.

I motored to a vacant spot on the dock and cut the engine. Craig met me there. I threw him a line and he tied her up to the dock.

"Anyone on board?" he asked as he hurried over the rail.

"Not that I can tell. I haven't searched her. I just called out, but got no answers."

We exchanged worried glances as Craig reached for the hatch door. I bit my lip as I followed him down the steps to the main salon.

"Ronnie? Jake?" I called.

No answer. Everything looked normal. There was no sign of a struggle. Nothing overturned. Nothing broken. Craig checked all the cabins. There was no one on board.

I made my way through the galley and spotted the note stuck to the refrigerator. Ronnie had scribbled it in a hurry, by the looks of it. It read:

Rick from Caper and Lawless called.
They found Lance, but there's a problem.
I have to get there right away. Ronnie.

I pulled the note from under the magnet and headed for the main salon to show it to Craig.

"They've gone to Mexico," I said, handing him the note.

"What? Why?" he asked. He read the note, then handed it back to me.

"They probably caught a flight to Cabo. That's where

Caper and Lawless were headed. I wonder what sort of problem it is they've run into?" I asked.

Craig picked his cell phone up from the coffee table. "If they'd kept this with them, we could have called to see where they are."

I frowned. Craig was right. We couldn't know for sure they were in Cabo. They could be anywhere. We had no way of knowing unless they contacted us.

"Well, the good news is that they're okay. I was worried someone may have taken them."

"I know. Me too," Craig said, reading my mind.

The short days of January meant it was dark by the time we were ready to set off for home. Craig led the way in the Sea Ray and I followed.

By the time we tied up to our dock, retrieved the puppy from Uncle Doug and finally settled into our house, I was exhausted.

"I guess all we can do now is wait," I said, as I searched the refrigerator for something quick and easy to fix for a late dinner.

Craig eased up behind me and peered into the illuminated box. "How about leftover spaghetti?"

"Sounds great. I'll heat it up. You want a salad?" I asked.

"Sure. I'll set the table."

At two in the morning, the ringing phone startled me out of a deep sleep. Craig reached over to the nightstand to pick it up. Most calls at this hour were from the hospital for some sort of emergency.

"This is Doctor Matthews," I heard him mumble into the phone.

I closed my eyes and attempted to drift back to sleep.

"Ronnie? Is that you?" he said, more alert this time.

I rolled over and turned on the lamp.

"Where are you?" he asked.

I listened with anticipation as he tried to get information.

"Wait a minute. Slow down. Say that again," he said, fumbling around the nightstand for a notepad and pen. He couldn't find one. He looked at me and mimicked writing in the air. I understood his sign language. I jumped out of bed and grabbed a pad and pen from the desk and handed it to him.

"Okay. Okay. Now, tell me how to get there from the airport," Craig said, scribbling something illegible on the paper I'd given him. He's joined the ranks of the top doctors with the worst penmanship in the world. Only he and a few well-trained pharmacists can actually decipher what he writes.

I watched his face as he listened to Ronnie's instructions. His chin dropped and he gave me a look as if he'd just learned a massive meteor was headed for Earth.

"Repeat that," he said. "How much?"

I scooted around to see what he wrote.

"How many zeros are we talking about? Two? Three? Three zeros? Okay. I think we can—"

His eyes nearly popped out of their sockets. "Each? How many are there? Ten?"

I watched him jot TEN THOUSAND on the paper, and then in bold letters, he printed CASH. I searched his face for a clue.

He glanced at the clock on the nightstand next to the bed. "I don't know. We'll get there as soon as we can. It may take some time to come up with the money. I don't suppose I can call you there. No, I didn't think so. Hang tight. The cavalry is on the way," he said, and then hung up the phone.

"What? What?" I asked, anxious to find out what that was all about.

Craig looked over the words he'd written. "They're all fine."

I waited for the rest. "But?"

"They're all in jail in Cabo."

"Jail? What for?"

"She didn't say. But one of the policemen said they could expedite their release for a thousand dollars—each," he explained.

"Each? And there's how many?"

"Ten. Ten thousand dollars—cash. They don't take traveler's checks and she said they definitely don't take credit cards. Surprise, surprise."

I stared at the figure on the paper. "We don't have ten thousand dollars. Do we?"

Craig shook his head. "Not that we could get our hands on by tomorrow morning."

Craig started calling in favors from other doctors in order to find someone to cover for him at the hospital until we could return. I told him I could go by myself. He scoffed. "Yeah, right. I'm gonna send my wife to a Mexican jail with ten thousand dollars in cash by herself. Think again." I was relieved he was insistent. I didn't want to go by myself.

I rang Uncle Doug's doorbell at seven in the morning. He answered the door in his robe, with a glass of orange juice in one hand.

"Let me guess. You want to borrow a cup of sugar?" he asked, knowing full well that my requests for favors never amounted to anything so trivial.

"Ten thousand dollars? Cash? What do I look like? The U.S. Mint?" Uncle Doug complained, stomping across the kitchen to retrieve a slice of toast.

"Lance Oakhurst will pay you back, with interest, if you want. He's good for it. The guy's got a six-figure salary," I told him.

Uncle Doug sat down across from me and buttered his toast. "How do you get mixed up with these people? You seem to have a knack for finding trouble," he said.

"I know. I'm sorry. I wouldn't ask if it weren't really important, Uncle Doug. Ronnie's not safe. We've got to get her out of there," I insisted.

"Maybe that's the safest place for her right now. Behind bars. Seems like the bad guys would want to avoid the jail."

Aunt Arlene glared at him.

"What?" he whined in self-defense.

"You know what. The man will pay you back. You can't let that poor girl sit in some Mexican jail," Aunt Arlene scolded.

"This isn't fair. Two against one."

Aunt Arlene crossed her arms over her chest. She was not going to back down.

"Okay. Okay," Uncle Doug surrendered. "The bank doesn't open until nine. Can I finish my breakfast in peace, please?"

I smiled and hugged him. "Thank you, Uncle Doug. You're the best."

I gave Aunt Arlene a hug and headed for the door. "Oh, one more thing," I said, stopping in the doorway. "We'll probably be gone a couple days. I'll drop the puppy off when I come by to pick up the money."

"Puppy? Wait a minute—" Uncle Doug started.

"That'll be fine, honey," Aunt Arlene said, smiling.

* * *

Our plane touched down late that afternoon. We exchanged just enough cash to cover taxi fares and a couple of meals. We didn't plan to stay in Mexico long.

I was sure we would be killed no less than three times on the taxi ride to the jail. The driver sped down the narrow road with one hand on the wheel and the other arm draped over the back of the passenger seat. He spent most of the time turned around, talking to us. I think he was practicing his English. He didn't get many fares that wanted to go to the jail. He was curious.

I had two semesters of Spanish in high school, and all I can remember is how to count to ten and the days of the week. Craig knows just a little more than I do, but most of the phrases he uses are related to his work at the hospital. Where does it hurt? How long have you had this pain? Do you have insurance?

We finally found a policeman who spoke more English than we did Spanish. When we told him we were there for Ronnie Oakhurst, he knew exactly where to take us. He led us to a tiny room with bare walls and a rickety table in the middle. Four unmatched, beat-up old chairs surrounded the table. We waited there for 15 minutes before the policeman returned with another officer. They sat across from us and smiled.

"You have something for us?" the new policeman asked.

Craig removed a bundle of money from his jacket pocket and set it on the table.

Their smiles faded. "American money?" one of them questioned.

Craig nodded. "It would not have looked good for us to try to exchange this much money at the airport. You can exchange it easily enough."

They looked at each other, and then nodded with satisfaction. Their smiles returned.

"Now. You have something for us?" I asked.

We were reunited with Ronnie and the other nine prisoners. The bribe-taking policemen led us down a narrow corridor and through some sort of maintenance room. He opened a door that led outside, peered out to see that no one was around, then motioned for us to proceed through the door into the side alley. We scrambled through the door as quickly as we could, anxious to get as far away from the place as possible. Gary stopped short of the doorway, looking at the policeman. "My truck?"

The policeman grinned. He pulled a set of keys from his pocket and handed them to Gary. He poked his head out the door. "Two blocks that way," he said, pointing down the alley.

"Gracias," Gary said, then stepped through the exit.

The policeman slammed the door and left the twelve of us standing in the alley, wondering what to do next.

"Why'd they send us out this way?" I wondered out loud.

Rick chuckled. "Because Officer Juan there doesn't want the official bribe-takers to know he's cutting in on their action. I think he's starting his own enterprise. Pretty good take—ten grand."

"I'd say so," Craig agreed.

We slowly wandered out of the alley to the main street that ran along the front of the jail. The crew of *The Dream Catcher* caught a taxi back to the airport. They'd decided they'd let the owner of the boat deal with the Mexicans to get it back. They just wanted out of the country. Lance's crewmembers had the same sentiments. Finally, Rick,

Gary, Lance, Ronnie, Jake, Craig, and myself were the only ones left standing in the dim light of a street lamp.

"Well, heck. This has been fun," Gary said. "My truck's parked two blocks that way. Why don't we all go grab a bite to eat? Then I'll give you folks a ride to the airport."

I grimaced. "Eat?" I asked, recalling the last time I'd had a meal in Mexico. I had sworn I never would again.

"You'll be fine. Just don't drink the water," Rick assured me. "That's where you get into trouble. No ice, either."

Gary took a step off the curb, and the rest of us had started to follow, when it happened. The explosion was enormous. The force of the blast sent us flying through the air. I remember landing hard on my side and rolling the rest of the way across the street, finally stopping only because I hit the curb.

I raised my head to see the jail engulfed in flames. The heat nearly scorched my face. I looked around at the others. "What happened?" I asked, moaning.

Craig rose to his feet and took my arm. "Are you okay?" he asked, helping me to my feet.

"I think so. How about you?"

"So far, so good. How about the rest of you guys?"

Slowly, everyone managed to stagger to their feet and inspect their limbs. Nothing appeared to be broken.

"Come on. We better get out of here, quick," Gary said, herding us toward his truck.

We ran to the pickup and piled inside. Gary locked the doors and started the engine.

"What happened back there?" Lance asked, looking out the window at the flames shooting into the sky.

Rick cranked his head around to get a better look at the fire. "Looks like someone found out Ronnie was a guest in the jail. You guys sure you want to get on a plane with her?"

Chapter Twelve

The decision was unanimous to ride back to the States with Rick and Gary rather than risk an air disaster with Ronnie on board. We drove all night to get as far from Cabo as possible. By mid-morning, the sound of our stomachs growling was almost as loud as the V-eight engine in Gary's truck. We stopped in a small village with dirt streets and searched for a place to eat.

Over breakfast, Gary recounted the events of the past few days that eventually landed them all in jail. Apparently, Lance's group decided to come ashore their first night in town to have a few beers. They found a little bar not far from the waterfront, and started ordering rounds. By the end of the night, there were a hundred and fifty empty beer bottles stacked on their table. Sometime during the evening, they'd gotten into a debate about which was faster—a Mexican taxi or a Mexican police car.

I cringed and looked at Lance. "You didn't."

He gave me a guilty smile and nodded.

Rick laughed. "These guys are crazier than we are—and we've done some pretty crazy things. But we never got drunk and stole two cars in Mexico, one of which was a police car, and raced them on the beach at midnight."

"You've got to be kidding," Craig marveled.

"No kidding. They did it. That's how they landed in jail," Gary said.

Something still troubled me. "But why was *The Dream Catcher* adrift?" I asked.

Lance appeared to want to slide under the table. "No one ever taught me how to tie a proper knot," he confessed.

Jake dropped his fork on his plate. "You mean they trusted you to tie up that . . . that very expensive boat? Do you have any experience at all?"

Lance shook his head. "It was just the first of many poor decisions made that night. I can't say any more that that."

I felt sorry for Lance. I decided to get him out of the spotlight. I turned my attention to Gary. "What about you? How'd you get arrested?" I asked.

"We got into town and found *The Dream Catcher* first thing. Only problem was the police had a guard on it. We wanted to look around—you know, see if there were any clues on board about where Lance might be," Gary explained.

"Anyhow, we waited until the guard dozed off, then we snuck on board. Ran right into a little party the . . . what would you call him? Chief of police? Anyhow, he and his girlfriend were having a good time. He greeted us with a machine gun aimed at our faces. Next thing we knew, we were in jail, and Lance and his buddies were our cell-mates," Rick continued.

"That explains your trip to the jail," Craig said. Then he

looked at Ronnie. "But you were supposed to come bail them out. What happened?"

Rick shook his head. "She's crazier than the rest of them put together."

"I am not," Ronnie protested.

"You show up with a half-dozen credit cards and you think they're gonna let us out?" Rick sniped.

"Everyone takes credit cards these days," Ronnie defended.

"Not for bribes, honey," Gary said.

"I didn't know it was a bribe. I thought it was a fine."

I waved a white napkin over the table. "Okay. Okay. Truce. That shouldn't have landed her in jail," I said.

Rick rolled his eyes. "No, but when the Mexicans laughed at her credit cards and tried to toss her out, little Miss 'Kung Fu' there decided to do her Bruce Lee impression. Took six policemen to finally get her caught and locked up. They took Jake, too."

Gary smiled and pointed at Ronnie. "She's good. I could use her in that martial arts flick we've got coming up."

Ronnie slipped two inches in her seat. She smiled, but the embarrassment showed on her face.

"She rolled pretty good last night when that bomb went off, too. Did you see her? As good as that little stunt-gal we worked with on the last film. I just have to get her in the union," Gary continued.

Rick glared at him over his glass of milk. "She won't take direction from you. She won't take direction from anyone."

Lance laughed. "You got that right. Must be all that red hair."

Jake noticed Ronnie's silence and leaned over to her. "You okay?"

She nodded. "I'm fine. Can we go now? I just want to get out of this country."

I raised my hand to catch Lance's attention. "Wait. The other question that still hasn't been answered is why Ronnie wasn't told about the change in the departure time from Long Beach."

Lance shot me a puzzled look. "No one told her?"

Ronnie shook her head. "Never heard a word," she said.

Lance shrugged his shoulders and met everyone's stares with eyebrows raised in a motion of self-defense. "A guy from the sponsor's headquarters called all of us the night before to let us know the time had changed. He told me he'd already talked to Ronnie, so I didn't bother to call her. I knew she'd halfway talked herself out of going on the trip. That's why I wasn't surprised when she didn't show up."

"Who called you?" I asked.

Lance looked at Jake. "I don't remember the guy's name, but you should know him. He's from World Motors," Lance said.

All our eyes turned to Jake. He assumed the self-defense posture that only moments before had been on Lance's shoulders. "Don't look at me," he defended. "Just because the guy said he was from World Motors doesn't mean they're the ones behind all this. It was probably one of those imposters from the other night—you know, Hollers or Pianalto."

Gary nodded in agreement. "Probably right. No use pointing fingers amongst ourselves. That'll only make things worse."

Jake relaxed and pushed his chair from the table. "Good. I vote we get out of here."

We all followed Jake's lead and got up from the table.

Jake paid the bill and we headed out the door. The seven of us crammed into the truck and braced ourselves for the long drive.

"If Rick's theory is right, then how'd they know Ronnie was in the jail?" I asked.

"That's easy," Rick said. "She called you, didn't she?"

Craig nodded. "Yeah?"

"Did she say where she was over the phone?" Gary continued.

"You mean our phones are bugged?" I said.

"Could be," Rick said. "But they don't have to actually bug your phones to listen to your conversations. Cell phone conversations can be monitored remotely, or they can set themselves up to look like telephone repairmen, up on a pole near your house."

Gary continued to check his side mirrors. I assumed he just wanted to make sure the trailer was okay, but he seemed nervous. I wondered if he was worried about someone following us. I started to watch the mirrors, too.

"One thing's for sure. Whoever is doing this has unlimited resources. I don't know how you're ever gonna beat them," Rick said.

"It'd help if we knew exactly who we were up against," Gary said.

"It's the oil companies. It's got to be," Ronnie concluded.

"Oh, that's a little bigger than a bread box. I think we have to narrow it down a bit. If we drew a diagram of the involved parties, we'd probably see oil companies at the top of the page, but we need to start at the bottom. We need to get our hands on the guy who pulls the trigger," Gary said.

In all the excitement of the past twenty-four hours, I'd

almost forgotten about the information I'd uncovered with my hacking tour of the oil company computers.

"I think we may have a clue there," I offered.

"How so?" Rick asked.

"Are you guys still on the case?" I asked.

Gary frowned. "We have be on the set in two days for that picture we told you about. I'm the stunt coordinator."

"You need to be there, but you won't need me for a couple days," Rick offered.

Gary nodded. "That's right. We could start with the bar-brawl scene first. Save the car scenes for later in the week."

Rick turned to face me. "What's the clue you think you have?"

Chapter Thirteen

By the time we reached the border, we were exhausted. We crossed without incident. We concluded that whoever had blown up the Mexican jail assumed they'd eliminated Ronnie for good. Since our release was "unofficial," and the policemen who'd let us go were likely killed in the explosion, there was no way anyone could know we'd escaped the blast. Even so, we agreed it would be a good idea to hide Ronnie somewhere safe. Rick and Gary had a place in mind. They said they could guarantee she'd be safe there.

After making a quick stop by our house to touch base with Uncle Doug and give him a check from Lance to repay the ten thousand dollar loan, Gary dropped Rick, Craig, and myself off at the airport in San Diego. He took Ronnie, Jake, and Lance to his "safe place," that even we couldn't know about. That's the reason the place was so safe, apparently. No one but Rick and Gary knew about it. They didn't tell anyone, even people they trusted.

The three of us trudged into the airport terminal and to the ticket counter. We bought three tickets to Reno, Nevada. That's the closest airport to Graeagle. Rick and Gary had come up with a plan that, hopefully, wouldn't land us all back in jail again.

We tried to sleep on the flight, but it was difficult. Reno greeted us with three inches of snow on the ground, and it was still falling. We rented a four-wheel-drive Blazer and headed west. Rick appointed himself the official driver. By the time we reached Hallelujah Junction, the snow was nearly a foot deep. Rick didn't slow down.

"I know you're a stunt driver and all that, but have you done much driving in snow?" I asked.

Rick didn't blink. "Grew up in it. My first car was a snowplow."

From the back seat, I glanced over to the front passenger seat and noticed Craig's death-grip relax a bit on the door armrest.

Rick took the turn onto Highway 70. I felt the Blazer slide sideways before he straightened it out. "I made sure we got a model with a roll bar. Wish we had helmets, though," Rick admitted.

Craig checked his seatbelt and grabbed the overhead handle.

Rick smiled at him. "Just kidding. Don't worry. I won't roll it."

Craig returned his smile. "I'll hold you to that."

The snow was two feet deep as we passed through Portola. The wipers were frantically trying to keep the windshield clear, but the blizzard conditions made it nearly impossible to see beyond the hood of the Blazer.

"How much farther?" Rick asked, squinting to see out the window.

"About fifteen miles, I think," I said, gripping the back of Craig's seat.

"Good. If this gets any worse, we're gonna have to pull over and wait for it to let up. I can't see the road."

"If you can't see the road, why don't we pull over now?" Craig asked.

"Because I can't see beyond the side of the road either. If I pull off, it might be right over a cliff," Rick said. "I'll just keep between the snowplow poles and we'll be okay."

"Great," Craig replied, not sounding too convinced.

We finally reached Graeagle and found the post office. The one good thing about the current blizzard was that it kept everyone at home and off the streets. Since it was after hours, even the postmaster was gone. The place was literally deserted.

I pulled the list of postal addresses out of my purse and handed it to Rick.

"Are you sure about this?" Craig asked, worried. "Tampering with mail. Isn't that a Federal offense? I think that's how they finally got Al Capone, isn't it?"

"Not exactly. Income tax evasion. Completely different," Rick replied.

I gave Craig a concerned look, then turned my eyes to Rick. "Should we be doing this?" I asked.

"You're not doing anything. Just go over there and pretend you're buying stamps out of that machine. Don't watch me. See no evil . . ."

I took Craig's arm. "Okay. We'll just be over here, buying stamps."

"Good. Keep an eye on the door. If you see anyone coming, give me a signal," Rick said.

Craig and I exchanged glances. "Accomplices. We're going to jail for sure," Craig said.

I nervously pressed buttons on the stamp machine, constantly glancing out the window to the street. Rick was busy picking the locks on the four boxes from the list of addresses I'd printed.

Rick finally stepped around the corner. "Come on. Let's go," he said, stuffing a bundle of envelopes inside his jacket.

We followed him out to the Blazer and piled in. I shook the snow out of my hair and peered over the seat to get a better look at the envelopes Rick had "liberated."

"We're lucky. This blizzard kept everyone away. Normally, those boxes would have already been emptied by now, I'm sure," Rick said.

He handed the envelopes to Craig and started the engine. "I'd feel better if we got out of here. I'd hate to be caught with this stuff right in front of the post office."

"Good thinking. Uncle Doug gave me the key to his place. Let's head over there and get some sleep. I don't think I can keep my eyes open another minute."

Craig offered to light a fire in the fireplace while I heated water to make instant hot chocolate I'd found in the cupboard.

"Where's the knob for the gas?" Craig called to me as I busied myself in the kitchen.

"Gas?" I questioned.

"Yeah. You know, to light the fire," he replied.

I smiled to myself. "No gas, honey. Gotta do it the old-fashioned way, with newspaper and kindling," I called back to him.

There was a brief moment of silence. "Where's the newspaper?" he finally asked.

I checked the fire on the stove, then walked into the living room. "I'll get some. The property management company makes sure there's always of supply of papers and firewood during the winter. The firewood's stacked out back, but I think the newspapers are in the garage."

I flipped the light on in the garage and glanced around for a stack of newspapers. I spotted the supply piled in the far corner. I grabbed one off the top and carried it back into the house. Amused, I read the headlines to Craig and Rick as though I were a news commentator reporting serious, earthshaking news. "Our top story tonight: Portola High School seniors hold a carwash to raise money for a senior trip to Disneyland. In other news, the mayor has agreed to appear at a public inquiry to answer questions as to why he has registered all his vehicles in the state of Oregon, when he obviously is a resident of California."

Craig chuckled. "What paper's that?"

"*Portola Reporter.* Lots different than the *Union Tribune,*" I noted. I pulled the small classified section out and handed it to Craig to build a fire. I wanted to save the rest of the paper to flip through later, just for kicks. First, we had important business to attend to.

We sorted through the envelopes for the four businesses. There were checks from five oil companies in addition to the original four that we already knew about.

I pulled another envelope out of the stack and gaped at the return address. "Look at this. Western Gas and Electric. It's gone even beyond the oil companies. The power companies are in on it too."

"Let me see that," Craig said, taking the envelope from me. He opened it and studied the check. "It's for thirty thousand. Didn't they just file for bankruptcy?"

I nodded in disgust. "Our bills go sky-high, and they're crying bankrupt while they're paying this kind of money to some fly-by-night mercenary group. Makes me sick."

Rick tossed another envelope on the pile. "Here's one from Madison Electric. Fifty thousand and change. Your friend Ronnie's in big trouble."

I felt a sinking feeling in my stomach. The odds seemed insurmountable that we'd beat what we were up against. "What do we do next?" I asked.

Rick gathered the envelopes back into a neat stack and placed them in the center of the table. "We stake out the post office. We need to find out who comes to claim the mail from those boxes. When they do, we follow. The more we know about them, the better."

"How are we going to do that? We can't just hang out all day in the post office. That'll look too suspicious," Craig said.

"We'll do it in turns. We'll wait outside. This is a tiny community. There won't be a lot of action. When someone goes in, one of us will follow. When you get inside, fumble with some keys like you're looking for the right one, but keep an eye on the boxes. If our guy goes to one of the four, then we know who to follow."

"When do we start?" I asked.

Rick glanced out the window. The storm was still heavy. "Tomorrow morning. It's late. I doubt anyone will be checking their mail tonight."

I checked my watch. It was nearly eight. "I found some soup in the pantry. Anyone interested in dinner?"

"I'm starved," Craig said.

"Sounds great. I'll put more wood on the fire," Rick offered.

After dinner, Craig and I retired to the master bedroom. Rick said he wanted to stay up to watch a sprint-car race on ESPN.

I brought the six-month-old *Portola Reporter* with me to bed. Craig read over my shoulder as I leafed through the pages. When I got to page four, a photo of a local resident standing next to his collection of off-the-wall costumes and props caught my attention. "Wait a minute," I said, pointing at the picture.

"What?" Craig asked.

I looked closer at the photo. "I've seen this before," I stated, jamming my finger on the page.

Craig studied the picture. "Sure. I remember that too. That's the big hamburger from those old commercials back in the late sixties or early seventies."

I shook my head. "No. I mean I've seen it recently."

Craig gave me a curious look. "You saw the hamburger?"

"No. I saw a picture of it. It was hanging on the wall in that shop Ronnie took me to the other day. Larry, the man we went to talk to about Ronnie's dad—he built it."

"He built Mayor McCheese?"

"Yes, and Big Mac too," I said, glancing down the page to find the story that accompanied the photo. "The question is, who is this guy, and what's he doing with it now?"

Craig placed his finger on the story. "There. His name's Cameron Boxer."

We both read the short article silently. The story indicated that Cameron Boxer was a local resident newly relocated to the Graeagle area from his previous home in the Hollywood Hills. He owned his own public relations and advertising firm, and hinted that he may be interested in featuring local talent in some upcoming commercials he had been hired to produce. The costumes appearing in the photos with him were purchased at auction over the years for his collection. He'd been gathering old items from studios since he was a young man in the late 1950's and early 1960's. He'd gathered so many that he had to build a huge warehouse on his property to store it all.

I slipped the page out from the rest and folded it over so the story and photo were the only items visible. "I don't think we need to stake out the post office tomorrow," I said, setting the newspaper down on the nightstand next to the bed. "This has got to be the guy we're looking for."

Craig reached over and switched off the lamp. "I think you're right. We'll show the story to Rick in the morning. I bet he'll agree."

I was out the minute my head hit the pillow. I don't know how long I'd been asleep when the banging on the bedroom door woke up both Craig and I.

"Get up! Come on! We've gotta get out of here!" Rick's voice boomed from the other side of the door.

"What's wrong?" Craig called out.

Rick burst through the door. "No time for questions. Come on. Now!" he reiterated.

We jumped out of bed and searched in the dark for our shoes. I laced mine up. Craig grabbed our jackets and tossed mine to me. I got one arm through when Craig grabbed my hand and led me toward the door. "Come on," he said, pulling me along.

"Wait," I said, rushing back to grab the newspaper page off the nightstand. We hurried down the hall to the living room.

Rick grabbed the stack of envelopes we'd taken and ran toward the fireplace, ready to toss them in the flames.

"Wait! What are you doing? We might need those for evidence," I demanded.

He opened the screen. "There is no way in the world any good can come from you or I being caught with these. We got the information we wanted."

Craig squeezed my hand. "He's right," he said.

Rick paused long enough to catch my expression. I knew he was right, too. I nodded. "Go ahead," I said.

Rick tossed the envelopes in the fire and closed the screen. Then, he grabbed his jacket and led us to the door. "Watch your step. Don't trip over this guy," he said, stepping over a man lying next to the woodpile.

I gaped at the seemingly lifeless man on the ground. "Oh my God. That's Pianalto," I blurted. "Is he dead?"

Rick unlocked the Blazer and jumped in the driver's seat. "No, he's not dead. But if we aren't gone by the time he wakes up, or when his partner gets back with reinforcements, we might be."

Craig and I raced to the Blazer. We jumped in just as Rick jammed it into gear and shoved his foot down on the accelerator.

"What happened back there?" I asked, as I buckled my seatbelt tight over my lap. Craig busied himself doing the same thing.

"I'd fallen asleep on the couch," Rick explained, checking the rear-view mirror. "I woke up and decided to put another log on the fire before I went to bed. I went out to the woodpile and surprised that guy sneaking around. There was another guy in a pickup parked on the street."

"Probably Hollers," Craig said.

"Maybe," I said. "Or, it could have been Cameron Boxer," I suggested.

Rick eyed me through the rear-view mirror. "Cameron Boxer?" he questioned.

"Yeah. We found an article about him in that paper we have. We think he's the guy we're after. There's a photo. Maybe you'll recognize him," I said, hopeful.

He shrugged his shoulders. "Don't know. Didn't get a good look at him. Anyhow, I cold-cocked the guy. His partner took off, but you can bet your stuntman union card he'll be back."

Rick adjusted the rear-view mirror. There were lights from a vehicle behind us. "You guys buckled in?" he asked.

We both double-checked. In unison, we said, "Yes."

Rick accelerated and took the next turn fast enough to send the Blazer spinning. We did a complete 360 before proceeding down the main highway. The lights followed us.

Rick glared at the rear-view mirror. "It's him," Rick hissed. "Hang on, guys."

We headed north. So did our tail. Rick drove fast. The guy behind us had trouble keeping up. He apparently wasn't a Hollywood stunt driver who'd grown up driving a snowplow. He hadn't caught up to us by the time we reached Blairsden, where the road we were on ended. The stop sign was coming up fast. Rick let his foot off the accelerator, but it was clear he didn't plan to stop. We slid around the corner, fishtailing the big Blazer. The lights behind us kept coming.

Luckily, the storm had passed and the road had recently been plowed, but it wasn't clear by any means. The plow left at least an inch of packed snow on the pavement. We kept our speed up as we headed back toward Portola.

Our tail was gaining confidence in his driving, and he seemed to be gaining on us. We approached an area with houselights off to the left. "What's up there?" Rick asked.

I searched my memory. The sign on the road said Delleker. "There's an old millpond up there. That's what that rise is," I said.

Rick spun the wheel and aimed the Blazer up the hill toward the pond. Our pursuer followed. Rick positioned the Blazer on the uphill side of the pond and stepped on the brakes. He studied the pond. "Is it frozen?" he asked.

"Probably. People skate on it in the winter," I confirmed.

"Is it deep?"

I had a sinking feeling. "Why?"

Rick didn't answer.

A dirt road skirted the pond on three sides. Rick turned the wheels downhill toward the pond. I grabbed the seatback.

The lights from the other truck got closer. Rick turned the wheel so we were moving across the face of the slope. It was too steep. The truck following us made the same move to try to catch us.

"Hang on," Rick said, turning the wheel. Almost in slow motion, the Blazer rolled over on its side, then on its roof, then on its side, then back on its wheels. We'd rolled completely over and landed right-side-up on the road that skirted the pond. The truck chasing us rolled, too, but it didn't stop on the road. It continued over the bank and landed upside-down on the ice.

Rick put the Blazer in low gear to get out of the deep snow and aimed it back toward the highway. We drove for ten minutes without saying a word. Craig glared at Rick the entire time.

Craig's scowl didn't go unnoticed by Rick. Finally, he broke the silence. "What?" Rick demanded.

"You promised you wouldn't roll it."

I put a hand on Craig's shoulder. He turned and smiled at me. "But I gotta admit, it was kind of fun," he said, grinning.

Chapter Fourteen

We huddled in a corner booth of an all-night diner on the edge of Reno. I spread open the page from the newspaper that featured Cameron Boxer and slid it across the table in front of Rick.

Rick studied the article. "Cameron Boxer? You think this is our guy?"

I nodded. "See that big hamburger there?" I said, pointing at the photo.

"Yeah?" Rick replied.

"A friend of Ronnie's built it for some commercials produced back in the late sixties. It was built in the machine shop where Ronnie's dad had done some work on his invention the same day he was killed in the explosion."

Rick continued reading the article, but didn't say anything.

"It's too much of a coincidence," I continued. "Cameron Boxer has a connection to Ronnie's dad through that shop, and now he runs this so-called 'advertising agency' in Graeagle. All these oil and energy companies are paying him megabucks. That guy you knocked out last night is one of the goons who tried to snatch Ronnie. How much you wanna bet he works for Boxer?"

Rick slid the paper back across the table to me. "Probably right. I've never heard of this Cameron Boxer. If he's been in the business as long as this article says, maybe Gary's heard of him."

Craig glanced at his watch. "What time's that flight out of here? I've had enough of the North Pole."

Rick slid out of the booth. "We should probably head for the airport. We have to drop the rental off."

Craig and I exchanged worried glances, which didn't go unnoticed by Rick.

"No need to mention that the Blazer has been involved in a roll-over incident," Rick said. "There wasn't any damage because the snow was so thick. Just let me do the talking. Okay?"

Craig and I nodded, glad to turn the entire matter over to Rick.

With barely six hours of sleep under his belt, I sent Craig off to work at the hospital. He could not finagle any more time off without offering our first-born or applying for a leave of absence.

I set the alarm to allow me one more hour of sleep before I had to head over to the Caper and Lawless office. Gary agreed to take the morning off from his movie work to bring Ronnie, Jake, and Lance in for a meeting.

Gary studied the photo of Cameron Boxer. "I don't recognize the guy," he said. He handed the article to Ronnie.

She gaped at the picture. "Oh my God. That's him," she blurted.

"Who?" I asked.

"Charlie Johnson. The sailor who tried to blow me up on his boat," she continued.

"What?" Lance asked, taking the paper from her so he could get a look at the fiend who tried to kill his sister. He examined the picture, scratching his head. "I remember this guy. I thought the name sounded familiar, but it's been a long time."

Ronnie focused her eyes on Lance. "You know him?"

Lance nodded. "He was a lot younger when I met him. He owned a couple of racing bikes and some pretty hot muscle cars. He had some machine work done at Harold's shop. Boy, he'd just picked up a real nice red and white Triumph the day. . . ."

We all waited for him to continue. Lance fell silent.

"The day what?" Ronnie pressed.

Lance's face took on a troubled look. "The day Dad died. I remember seeing it that day. I asked Harold about it. He told me Cameron Boxer had just bought it and wanted something modified on the exhaust system."

We all stared at Lance. "Do you remember who he worked for? He must have been making some pretty good money to afford all those expensive toys," Rick said.

Lance stared at the ceiling, searching his memory. "You know, come to think of it, he didn't work. He came out to California from Texas, where his father had made a fortune in the oil business. They owned a bunch of wells. Filthy rich."

"It would seem Cameron Boxer, the good son that he is, has worked hard to make sure the family business thrives," Gary said.

Jake had been quiet during most of the meeting. Finally, he spoke up. "So what happens now? How do we get this Boxer guy and his goons locked up so they leave Ronnie alone?"

Good question, I thought to myself. I'm sure Ronnie was wondering the same thing.

"Cameron Boxer has been in business a long time. He must be good to not have gotten caught. He's got to be afraid of Ronnie, because she can identify him as the man who tried to kill her," Gary explained. "If he gets any hint at all that we're onto him, he's gonna be gone in a flash. Your best bet now is to get Sam involved again. He might even bring in the Feds for help."

We all nodded in agreement. "I think you're right," I said.

Rick cleared his throat to get our attention. "I hate to spoil everyone's good mood, but the problem still isn't solved, you do realize," he announced.

I gave him a curious look, then suddenly grasped his meaning.

"Even if Cameron Boxer and his band of murderers are taken out of the picture, there's probably a dozen more waiting in line for the new business opportunity," Rick continued. "We can't lose sight of the fact that Boxer's success is due to the energy industry's determination to stay in power."

No matter how you looked at it, Ronnie's future seemed hopeless. We all turned our faces to Jake, the one man in the room who might have a chance to turn things around for her, if only he would.

He felt the weight of our stares. "Why are you all looking at me like that? My hands are tied."

Ronnie threw her hands in the air. "Fine. What are you

doing here, then? Why don't you pack up your toys and go back to your keepers in Detroit? I don't need you here. All you've managed to do is lead every one of Boxer's guys to my doorstep. If I didn't know any better, I'd say you were one of them."

Injured, Jake's pleading eyes fell on Ronnie's face. "Ronnie. Don't be this way. You know I'd do anything to keep you safe from—"

"Save it, Monroe. Just go away," she snapped, coldly.

"Ronnie," he begged.

"Go away," she hissed.

I couldn't help but feel bad for Jake, but Ronnie was right. If he wasn't willing to help her, then he needed to stay away from her to make it harder for the Cameron Boxers of the world to find her.

"Can I give you a ride to the airport?" I asked Jake.

He watched Ronnie's face for any sign of a change of heart. When he concluded that he was getting no stay of execution, he nodded to me. "Thanks. I could use a ride."

I dropped Jake off in front of the United terminal at the airport. "Sorry for the way things turned out," I said, with as much sympathy in my voice as I could manage.

"Not as sorry as I am," he replied as he started to close the passenger door.

"Jake," I said, stopping him from closing the door. "It's probably best if you don't try to contact Ronnie. You know, until. . . ."

"Until? Until what?" he snapped.

I didn't know how to answer. I shrugged my shoulders.

"Don't worry. I won't bother her," he said, then headed for the doors to the terminal.

* * *

I delivered Ronnie and Lance to the police station where Sam had arranged a meeting with two Federal agents who would be working with him on the arrest of Cameron Boxer and his crew.

After compiling a long list of charges made against Cameron Boxer, Sam looked at me. "As much as I hate to ask this, can you arrange to come with us to Graeagle?"

I couldn't believe my ears. "You want me to come along?" I asked.

"No, but you're a witness and you can ID some of these characters. I don't want to take a chance of picking these guys up and hauling them a thousand miles just to find out they're the wrong ones. Besides, we're gonna have to work with the local authorities up there. The more credible witnesses I have to back up my request to extradite them into my custody, the better."

I smiled. "I'm not only a witness, but now I'm a *credible* witness?"

Sam scowled at me. "Don't get smart. When can you be ready to go?"

Chapter Fifteen

Ronnie, Lance, and I sat in a quiet corner and watched the experienced police officers and Federal agents flesh out their plan for the big sting operation. We'd been instructed to meet the Plumas County sheriff at his home rather than at the police station, to avoid being spotted by Cameron Boxer or any of his employees.

"You know where all these people live?" Sam asked the local sheriff.

Sheriff Dino Santucci scoffed at the question. "I know where every resident of this county lives," he bragged. "And if I happen to forget one or two, I can have the address in five minutes."

Sheriff Santucci's big frame barely fit into the uniform stretched around his body. Not that he was fat, because I didn't think there was an ounce of fat on him. He was just big. I wondered why the county didn't provide him with a uniform of the proper size.

"And as far as you know, these three men—Boxer, Hollers, and Pianalto—haven't left the area?" Sam asked.

"Saw them myself this morning, having breakfast over at Perko's. They were having some kind of important meeting, looked like to me," Sheriff Santucci said. "I sent three of my men to stake out their houses after you called me. I expect a report any minute."

At that moment, the conversation was interrupted by a ringing telephone.

"Excuse me," Sheriff Santucci said, picking up the phone. "Santucci," he barked into the receiver. "What've you got? All of them? Good. Stay put. We'll be there in twenty minutes."

Sam and the Federal agents watched the sheriff's face, hopeful for good news.

"We got 'em. They're all over at Boxer's place. Doubles as his office, so that's their official workplace," Santucci said, pulling his big revolver out of its holster to check his bullets.

Sam and his men stood and proceeded to check their weapons. I got to my feet, ready to go.

"Where do you think you're going?" Sam asked.

"I thought—"

"You three are staying right here. The last thing I need is a bunch of civilians getting in the way of a potentially hazardous arrest."

"But—"

"But nothing. Right here. Understand?"

I nodded and sat back down next to Ronnie.

One of Sheriff Santucci's clerks stayed with us at his

house while the army of authorities set out to capture the bad guys. He produced a deck of playing cards and proceeded to shuffle them.

"Anyone for a game of fish?" he asked.

After a dozen hands of every card game the four of us could recall from our teenage years, Sheriff Santucci's telephone rang. The clerk grabbed it and listened carefully to the voice at the other end. "Ten-four!" he blurted into the phone, then hung up.

"They got 'em," he announced. "I gotta take you all down to the station so you can ID the perps."

I smiled at the clerk's enthusiasm over what must be the most excitement to hit this community since the high school math teacher's daughter chained herself to a buoy in the middle of Lake Davis to prevent the poisoning of the pike fish.

I wasn't prepared for what I saw when we arrived at the small police station. An EMT was trying to get Sheriff Santucci to sit down long enough to apply a bandage to his bleeding arm. Santucci kept swatting him away like an annoying insect. "I'm okay, Elvis. Just a flesh wound," he insisted.

"It's a gunshot wound, Sheriff. I gotta clean it," the EMT insisted.

"In a minute. Now go see about those other fellas over there," Santucci said, pointing to three men huddled around a small desk, applying pressure to various wounds inflicted on their bodies.

Sam waved Ronnie, Lance, and I over to the desk he was perched on. A medic was cleaning a gash in his forehead. He winced at the stinging of the antiseptic on his open flesh.

"Are you okay?" I asked, staring at the cut, which was still producing enough blood to require a mopping up every few seconds.

"Ouch!" Sam exclaimed, trying to shrink from the cotton swab doused with something that smelled like it could kill every form of bacteria ever discovered.

"What happened?" I asked, glancing around the room at a half-dozen bleeding men in uniforms.

Sam pushed the medic's hand away from his head and took over the task of applying pressure to his wound. "They resisted arrest."

"I guess so," I said. "Was anybody seriously hurt?"

Sam shook his head. "Just a few cuts and scratches. Maybe a few stitches. We were lucky."

"Where are Boxer and his men?" Ronnie asked nervously.

"They're locked in a holding cell. When we're done here, I'm gonna have you take a look at them. Make sure we got the right guys. Then we're on our way home," Sam explained.

News of the arrest spread like wildfire in the small community. By the time we returned to San Diego, every major network was reporting the arrest of the group of men implicated in the murders and attempted murders of several inventors across the country over a time period of nearly 35 years.

By the end of the second day of his incarceration, Cameron Boxer had not uttered a single word about the charges against him. Hollers and Pianalto were equally as tight-lipped. I imagined they were more afraid of the ramifications of exposing the entities that supported their business than the penalties imposed on them by the law.

Ronnie had been whisked off into a witness protection program until all the major players could be rounded up and an attempt was made to hold them accountable for their crimes.

Craig and I made an effort to return to some normal semblance of life. We were in the back yard, playing with the puppy, which had managed to double in size since he came to live with us.

"Uncle Doug says if we don't name this puppy by the end of the week, he's going to do it for us," I said to Craig.

"Uh-oh. I bet we won't like the name he comes up with."

"Probably not. He suggested Dogzilla," I said, chuckling.

The cordless phone rang on the patio table. I jumped up to answer it. "Hello?"

"Devonie? This is Jake," he said.

"Hi Jake. How are you?"

"Fine. Have you seen Ronnie?" he asked.

"No, Jake. I don't even know where she is. You know you can't have any contact with her," I reminded him. I was surprised he even made the attempt.

"I know, but now that Boxer is locked up—"

"Right. Boxer's locked up. The hornet's nest has been hit with a stick. You think that makes Ronnie's situation better?"

There was a long silence on the other end of the line. Finally, he spoke. "Devonie. If by chance you see or talk to her, just tell her I asked about her and hope she's doing okay."

"I will," I assured him.

"And tell her I love her," he quickly added.

"Okay, Jake."

*   *   *

Craig ran into the master bathroom and grabbed my arm while I brushed my teeth. "You've gotta see this," he said, as he pulled me down the hall to the living room, where the nightly news blared from the television.

I wiped the toothpaste from my chin and sat on the edge of the sofa. I watched the replaying of the horrible events as they played out earlier in the day. As Boxer, Hollers, and Pianalto were being escorted into the courthouse, a military-looking helicopter appeared from out of nowhere. A sniper in the chopper opened fire on the men, striking them all down on the front steps of the courthouse. In 10 seconds it was all over, and the helicopter disappeared as quickly as it had appeared. The reports had been verified. It was official. Cameron Dean Boxer, Archibald Quincy Hollers, and Antonio Vincent Pianalto were pronounced dead at the scene.

Chapter Sixteen

Not more than 20 minutes after hearing the news about the assassination, our phone rang. It was Sam.

"Devonie, have you seen Ronnie?" he asked, sounding almost out of breath.

"Ronnie? No. Don't tell me you've lost her," I said, dreading his response.

"She's missing. Just disappeared. No one saw anything. I was hoping maybe she'd try to contact you," he explained.

"No. Have you checked with her brother?" I asked.

"Yeah. Tried him first. He's madder than a cat with a sock on its head."

"So you think she took off on her own? Not taken by those guys who killed Boxer and his gang?" I asked.

"At this point, we don't know. We're hoping she just saw the news and got scared. Took off and found her own hiding place," Sam said, trying to sound hopeful.

"Well, she has no home to go back to. Lance is her only

family. Jake is back in Detroit. I doubt she'd look him up. Last time I saw them together, he wasn't earning any points with her," I said.

"Anyone else you can think of?" Sam asked. "Anyone she may have mentioned who might hide her out?"

I searched my memory for anything she might have told me in passing. "I can't think of anyone she talked about enough that she'd trust her life to."

Sam made a half-growl, half-moan sound into the phone. I pictured him eating aspirin like candy. "Okay," he groaned. "If you hear anything, call me. Don't go playing Wonder Woman. I think we've got a dragon by the tail here, and no swords."

I told Craig about Sam's call as we climbed into bed. He eyed me closely as I told him about Ronnie's disappearance. I noticed his strange stare.

"What's wrong?" I asked.

"What are you planning?" he replied.

"Me? Nothing. Why?"

He laughed. "Yeah, right. Nothing. I don't think you're capable of doing nothing."

"Am so," I defended.

He just grinned at me. He wouldn't look away. I felt like a bug in a glass jar. He knew me so well.

"Okay. So maybe I'll just ask around tomorrow. Maybe her friend Larry knows something. Or maybe I'll call Jack Pearle. Couldn't hurt," I said.

Craig switched off the lamp on the nightstand. "Just promise you'll be careful. Okay?"

"I'm always careful," I said. Then I thought about the events of my life over the past three years and wondered how I could make such a claim.

* * *

I called Larry's shop and asked him if he'd heard from Ronnie in the last couple of days. He hadn't heard a word from her.

I called Jack Pearle, but could not get an answer. I finally decided to take a drive to his shop. When I arrived, the place didn't look much different than the first time I'd been there. The doors were all closed. I knocked, but no one answered. I stepped up to the window and cupped my hands over the glass to see inside. The place was empty. All the machines were gone. The workbenches were bare. I stepped back and double-checked that I had the right shop. The number stenciled on the door was definitely the right one. I gazed around the complex, confused. I wandered across the driveway to an open door where I saw activity inside.

"Excuse me," I said, catching the attention of a man busily applying some sort of fiberglass resin to the underside of a small boat.

He stood straight and removed the mask from his face. "Can I help you?" he asked.

"I'm looking for Jack Pearle. Have you seen him?"

The man glanced past me, toward the door that used to belong to Pearle Manufacturing. "That's his shop over there," he said, nodding in the general direction of Jack's shop.

"I know, but it seems to have been closed down," I said.

"Huh?" he replied.

"It's empty. No machines. No nothing," I explained.

The man set down his tools and shook his head. "Can't be. He was here, big as life, yesterday."

"Well he's not here now," I reiterated.

The man put his mask down on a bench and marched across the driveway to Jack's door and tried the knob.

When he realized it was locked, he knocked. "Jack's late coming in most days," he said, waiting for something that wasn't going to happen. "Like he always says, 'Jack doesn't tick for time. Time ticks for Jack.'"

I motioned toward the window. "Take a look for yourself. It's empty."

He peered through the window. "Well I'll be danged. I swear it was business as usual yesterday. He had to have moved everything out last night."

All the way home, I racked my brain to come up with an answer to where Jack Pearle might have disappeared to, and why.

When I arrived home, I tossed a pile of mail on the table in the foyer, set my purse on the kitchen table and rummaged through a stack of business cards, looking for the one Jake Monroe gave me. I dialed the direct line for his office. As I listened to his voice-mail announcement, I carried the cordless phone through the house to the back door to let the puppy in. I didn't have the heart to lock him in his kennel, which didn't seem big enough for a dog his size. I decided he should have free run of the back yard. He happily bounded in through the open French doors and licked my feet. I giggled and patted him on the back.

When Jake's recording beeped in my ear, I left him an urgent message to call me as soon as he got in. I didn't tell any details of the emergency over the phone. When three hours had passed, and he had not returned my call, I decided to try calling him again. I pressed the o button halfway through his voice-mail message so I could speak to the company switchboard operator. After being transferred to a half-dozen different departments, I finally determined that Jake was not anywhere in the plant. Though no one told me so, I got the impression that his absence was not planned. He just didn't show up for work today.

I sat down at the kitchen table, frustrated. The familiar sound of toenails clicking on the tile floor distracted me. The puppy trotted to me, carrying an envelope in his mouth.

"What've you found?" I asked, pulling the paper out of his slobbery grip. I wiped it dry. It was our phone bill. It must have fallen off the table in the entryway when I tossed the stack of mail on it. The puppy just stared at me, wagging his tail.

"What?" I asked, curious about his eagerness.

He let out a bark. I looked at the envelope, then back at the dog. I opened the bill. One of Ronnie's calls to Jake Monroe's home was listed among our calls for the month.

I gaped at the huge puppy at my feet and recalled those silly episodes of "Lassie" where the brilliant collie communicated complicated messages to her dim-witted humans. I took the puppy's head in my hands and kissed him on the top of his nose. "You're a genius!" I said, dialing Jake's number.

He picked up on the second ring. "Ronnie?" he blurted into the phone, sounding as though he were expecting her call.

I hesitated a moment, surprised by his greeting. "No. Devonie," I finally said.

"Oh. I saw your number and thought maybe Ronnie was at your house," Jake replied.

"Why would she be here? She's supposed to be in hiding."

Jake was silent.

"You know she's missing?" I pressed.

After a long pause, he finally spoke up. "She called me

last night, after the news of the shooting in front of the courthouse. She was scared. She said she wanted to run away."

I felt a dull headache starting at the base of my skull. I squeezed my eyes closed and rubbed the back of my head. "What did you tell her?" I asked.

"I told her to stay put. She was safe where she was. She didn't buy it. If the authorities couldn't protect those low-life murderers, how could they protect her?" he asked. Then, after a moment of thought, he added, "She's probably right."

"Did she say anything about where she was going?"

"No. Just that she'd call me when she felt it was safe. I think she was at a payphone. She's paranoid about using phones now. Calls are so easy to trace."

"What else? Did she say anything about what she was thinking?"

"Just that she thought she might reconsider an offer someone made her months ago."

"Offer? You think she's talking about Jack Pearle's offer? A partnership?" I speculated.

"Maybe. She wouldn't elaborate."

"Because he's disappeared too," I added.

"What?"

"He's gone. Poof. All his equipment moved out of his shop in the middle of the night. No one at the complex knows anything about it," I explained.

"This is crazy. I'm booking a flight out there tonight," Jake insisted.

"And do what? Go where? We don't know where either of them are," I said.

"What about those guys who hid her before? You know, Caper and Lawless?"

"I tried to call them. They're on location in South America. Won't be back in the country until next month."

"I have to do something. I can't just sit here."

"There's not much you can do, Jake," I said, fully aware that there actually *was* something he could do, but was not willing to. But the more I thought about it, the more I realized that even if Jake did take Ronnie's engine to the decision makers at World Motors, he'd probably never get them to agree to build it.

"Maybe there is something I can do," Jake said, as if he'd just come up with an idea.

"What?" I asked.

"I can't say. It's probably crazy, but it's a shot. I gotta go. I'll keep in touch," he said, then the line went dead.

"Jake?" I repeated into the phone. Too late. He was gone.

Weeks passed. No word from Jake or Ronnie. I tried everything I could think of to locate Jack Pearle. I got his home address from one of the other tenants in the industrial complex where his shop used to be. He hadn't been home since the night he loaded up all his machines.

I kissed Craig and sent him off to work early on a Monday morning. Albert had an appointment to get his puppy shots at the veterinarian's office at nine. Finally, the puppy had a name: Albert, as in Einstein. I told Craig the story of how he brought me the telephone bill and we both agreed he deserved a name that reflected his obvious intelligence. I think we were like those parents who are sure their babies are far ahead of all the other infants their age.

Albert sat up in the back seat of the Explorer and gazed intently out the window at the passing sights. I smiled at him in the rear-view mirror. "Maybe next time, I'll let you drive," I said. He gave me a look that made me wonder if he actually understood what I told him.

I slowed to a stop at a signal and waited for the light to turn green. A workman was busy putting the finishing touches on a new billboard across the intersection. I read it, and my heart picked up an extra beat. *Fed up with the high cost of energy? Don't get mad—get independent.*

I scribbled the telephone number from the billboard on a piece of scrap paper I dug out of my purse. Cars behind me honked because the light had turned green. I finished writing, tossed the pen and paper on the seat next to me, and pressed my foot on the accelerator.

I hurried home and rushed to the phone. I punched in the number and waited. I was greeted with a recording that requested I leave my name and telephone number, and someone would call me back. I breathlessly blurted my information into the phone, then hung up. I frantically searched for Jake Monroe's card and called his office. Instead of hearing his voice, or even his recorded voice-mail message, I was put right through to the switchboard operator.

"Can I please speak to Jake Monroe?" I requested.

"I'm sorry. Mr. Monroe is no longer with World Motors," she said.

"What? When did this happen?" I asked, baffled.

"I can't say any more than that. I'm sorry. Is there someone else who can help you?" she asked.

Stunned, I shook my head. "No, thanks."

I tried Jake's home phone, but there was no answer there, either.

I sat at the table and tried to think of what to do next. I didn't want to wait for someone to return my call. That could take days for all I knew. I pulled the phone directory from a drawer and found the section for outdoor advertising. I called all the billboard companies in the area and finally found the firm that owned the one I'd seen on my way home from the vet's office. After some convincing, the girl surrendered the address of the client who commissioned the billboard. They were, after all, an advertising agency. She had no special instructions to withhold information from potential clients. I thanked her and hung up the phone.

I gathered up my purse, let Albert out into the back yard, and rushed to the front door. I yanked it open and nearly jumped out of my skin when the face of the man standing on the porch startled me.

"Jake! What are you doing here?"

Chapter Seventeen

With no time for explanations, I dragged Jake out to the Explorer parked in the driveway and told him to get in. On the way to the address I'd received from the billboard company, I told him my theory. I suspected that Jack Pearle was the man behind the message on the billboard, because I'd heard him say it before—the first time I met him.

"What are you doing here, anyway?" I asked him as we cruised down the freeway.

"I have to help her. I don't care what happens to me. It's my fault she's in such deep trouble. If I hadn't encouraged her to file that patent . . ."

"But how can you help her? You don't even work for World Motors anymore."

"How'd you find out?" he asked.

"I tried to call you this morning. What happened?"

"It's a long story. Let's just say I tried to get Ronnie's engine on the drawing board. Once I realized floating the idea was like trying to launch a lead balloon over the Grand Canyon, I also grasped the reality that my life wasn't worth a plug nickel. I dropped out of sight, and the next thing I knew, I was on a flight to the last place I'd seen Ronnie."

We pulled into the industrial complex and searched for the unit number I'd noted with the address.

"There. Unit C," Jake said, pointing out the window toward the huge building.

I parked the Ford and we both jumped out, hurrying for the door. It was locked. We could hear pounding and machine noises inside. I pushed a button next to the door that was marked RING BELL and waited. I glanced up and noticed the security camera aimed at us. I nudged Jake and pointed at it. "Smile for the camera," I said.

We waited nearly a full minute before the door slowly eased open. Jack Pearle reached his hand out and pulled me in by the arm. Jake followed.

"I got your phone message this morning," Jack said. "I tried to call you back, but there was no answer."

I nodded. "I couldn't wait. I tracked you down through the billboard company," I explained.

Troubled, Jack made a note to call the advertising company. "I don't want them giving out this address."

Jack squinted at Jake. "Who's he?"

"Jake Monroe. I'm a friend of Ronnie's. Is she here?"

Jack shook his head. "No."

At that moment, Ronnie appeared from behind a closed door. "It's okay, Jack. He's a friend," she said, stepping to the center of the small office we stood in. The relief on Jake's face was unmistakable. He rushed across the room and wrapped his arms around her. She melted in his embrace.

Jack's eyes met mine, and his eyebrows lifted. "Guess they're friends," he said, grinning.

After the reunion, Jack and Ronnie took us on a tour of the plant. Dozens of crates were stacked near some sort of loading dock. "What are they?" I asked.

"Generators," Ronnie announced, proudly. "Like the one I built for my house. We have a website on the Internet and put up those billboards. We've got orders for hundreds of them, so far."

Jake and I exchanged worried glances. "And how long do you think it'll take before they find you here and put a stop to your enterprise?" Jake asked. "Look how easy it was for us to find you."

Ronnie stuck her chin in the air. "Then they'll stop us. But not before we get as many as we can of these units out to the people. Once it starts, there'll be no stopping it. I may not live to see it happen, but at least I'll die knowing I started something big—really big."

Jake turned his attention to Jack. "And you're willing to risk your life, too?"

"Darn right I am," Jack assured him. "Someone's got to have the guts to stand up to them."

Jake took Ronnie's hand and led her to a chair. "Sit down," he said. "I want to help. I have an idea. It's a long shot, but it just might work."

We all perked up our ears to hear Jake's plan.

"I tried to sell your engine to my bosses at World Motors. They shot me down," he explained. "After making that daring move, I knew there was no way to turn back. I approached every major auto manufacturer in Detroit. They all had the same reaction. The same force controls them all."

Worry lines appeared in Ronnie's forehead. "Then you're in as much danger as I am," she concluded.

"Looks that way," he confirmed. "But I have an idea. Japan."

"Japan?" Ronnie questioned.

"Your operation here is not big enough to take off. They'll stop you before you get enough units out there. They'll stomp out your little spark of a flame before it can turn into a blazing wildfire," Jake said.

"So, what's in Japan?" Ronnie asked.

I was already up to speed with Jake's suggestion.

"Competition," I offered.

Jake pointed a finger at me. "Exactly. And auto companies that are much more willing to develop and market cars with superior efficiency and cleanliness. I don't know why they seem not to be intimidated by the oil and gas industry, but they always lead the pack when it comes to new technologies in fuel efficiency. Maybe it's that kamikaze mindset left over from the war."

Jack pulled a chair up to a desk and sat down. "So what are you suggesting?"

"We put together three demo engines. Ship them over to Japan. I've got contacts with the three major manufacturers over there. I've already contacted them. They're all very interested."

I smiled. *It could work.* "And if the engines perform as we all know they will, they'll probably develop a new model—the 'free-to-run' car," I suggested. "There'd probably be a pretty good market for it."

Jake shook his head. "We don't want some new little weird-looking car that looks like it came out of a bad Woody Allen movie. This engine doesn't have the weight restrictions that we see with electric cars. It can go right into existing models—models that already have a huge following. Imaging how many Honda owners would trade in their V-six Accords for an identical car, equally priced, that delivers the same horsepower but doesn't cost anything to drive."

Jack slapped his hands on the desk. "American car makers wouldn't have a choice. If they want to stay in business, they'll have to follow Japan's lead. I don't care how dedicated the public is to buying American. When it comes to saving that much money, and that much pollution, and gaining that much independence, no one in their right mind would choose otherwise."

Ronnie's excitement turned to a worried frown. "But what if we go over there, and they turn out to be just like the car makers here? They can be intimidated. I don't care who they are. I've seen what these people can do."

Jake took her hands into his. "It's possible, I admit, but I think we have a pretty good chance. You said yourself that you're willing to risk your life to get this technology out to the people. This way, we have a better chance of getting that wildfire started before they can stomp it out. What do you say?"

Her frown turned into a smile. "How soon can we get three demo engines put together, Jack?"

Jack looked at his watch. "I've seen the drawings. We have all the equipment here to do it. I think we could have them ready to ship by next week."

Ten days later, Craig and I picked up Ronnie and Jake from the non-descript machine shop that was busily working to build as many 'free-to-run' generators as it could manage without drawing too much attention to itself. Jack stayed behind to make sure all the orders would be filled.

We dropped Ronnie and Jake at the San Diego airport. They had a flight out to Japan, and from there, Jake's contact, a man he trusted without hesitation, guaranteed their safety once in the foreign country.

We watched the plane take off and each said a little prayer that the trip would be successful. On the way home, Craig pulled into a gas station to fill the tank in my Explorer. I grimaced at the price posted on the sign. "Look at that. Two eighteen a gallon. This'll cost a fortune to fill," I complained.

Craig took a deep breath and turned his head my direction. Then, he beamed a huge smile. "No worries, honey. I have a feeling things are going to be changing for the better real soon."

A shiver of excitement raced up my spine. I felt the anticipation of what was in the works, and felt proud that I could say I played a small part in an event that would change the world.

Epilogue

Craig and I lounged in the comfort of our backyard, soaking up the last bits of warmth from the sun as it slowly dropped on the horizon, barely touching the surface of the Pacific. Albert, now fully grown, galloped around the yard, carrying a toy duck in his mouth. I sipped on a concoction I made in the blender—grapefruit and pineapple juice, fresh organic strawberries, and ice. As I perused the probate and foreclosure notices in the newspaper, Craig read the latest issue of *Popular Mechanics*.

"Listen to this!" Craig said, nearly dropping his fruit juice smoothie in his lap. He began reading from an article printed in the magazine. "'Last week, representatives from the top three Japanese auto manufacturers held a press conference to announce a new engine technology they plan to incorporate into their most popular models as early as next year. The companies admit that it's unusual, since they are in direct competition with one another, that they would join together in this daring move. When questioned about this strategy, they admitted that the engineer who designed the engine—who, surprisingly, is an American, and even more surprising, a woman—refused to sell the patent, but negotiated a deal which would allow the Japanese companies to use the technology in their products. The agreement requires that all three manufacturers participate, that the engine has to be offered as an optional feature on their top three selling models, and the price for a car with the engine must be the same or less than an otherwise equally-equipped model. Since the cost to manufacture the engine, once the initial start-up costs have been absorbed, is less than that of a conventional engine, the companies agreed to this rather unusual stipulation.'"

I smiled and took another sip through the straw. "She really did it. She pulled it off."

"Wait, there's more," Craig continued. "'Absent from the press conference was Ronnie Oakhurst, the woman who designed the technology. A member of our staff was able to catch up with her and get a brief interview. Miss Oakhurst is currently negotiating with another division of one of these Japanese automakers, a division that produces, among other things, generators. Apparently, the applications for this engine go far beyond just automobiles. One day, according to Oakhurst, every home in the free world will be completely independent from power utility companies. A generator, about the size of an existing air-conditioning unit, will be a standard fixture in every backyard. Unsightly webs of electrical power lines will be a thing of the past. Air pollution will be something our children only know about because they had to study it in history class. Everyone will be able to afford to heat and cool their homes, light their rooms, irrigate their crops, and run their businesses. With all the money people save from not having to support the lifestyles the oil company executives have grown accustomed to, they can actually afford to take time to enjoy their newfound freedom, newfound health, and an Earth that may regain some of the beauty that existed before the days when the burning of fossil fuel was necessary.'"

I closed my eyes and stroked Albert's velvety ears as Craig finished reading the article. I basked in the glow of hope, of the realization that some of the problems that came along with the wondrous advancements of the Industrial Revolution were on their way to being solved. I thought about Ronnie and the satisfaction she must feel, finally finishing what her father had tried to start so many years ago. *Wouldn't he be proud of her now?* It just went to show that one little person could accomplish great things, as long as that person had the determination, courage, and desire to make things better.